NEW 01/18

A DASH OF TROUBLE

LOVE SUGAR MAGIC

A DASH OF TROUBLE

ANNA MERIANO

WALDEN POND PRESS
An Imprint of HarperCollins*Publishers*

Sycamore Public Library
103 E. State Street
Sycamore, IL 60178

When cooking, it is important to keep safety in mind. Children should always ask permission from an adult before cooking and should be supervised by an adult in the kitchen at all times. The publisher and author disclaim any liability from any injury that might result from the use, proper or improper, of the recipes contained in this book.

Walden Pond Press is an imprint of HarperCollins Publishers. Walden Pond Press and the skipping stone logo are trademarks and registered trademarks of Walden Media, LLC.

A Dash of Trouble

Text copyright © 2018 by Cake Literary LLC
Illustrations copyright © 2018 by Mirelle Ortega
All rights reserved. Printed in the United States of America.
No part of this book may be used or reproduced in any manner whatsoever without written permission except in the case of brief quotations embodied in critical articles and reviews. For information address HarperCollins Children's Books, a division of HarperCollins Publishers, 195 Broadway, New York, NY 10007.
www.harpercollinschildrens.com

ISBN 978-0-06-249846-5

Typography by Sarah Nichole Kaufman
17 18 19 20 21   CG/LSCH   10 9 8 7 6 5 4 3 2 1
❖
First Edition

Sycamore Public Library
103 E. State Street
Sycamore, IL 60178

For my loving, sweet, magical family

CHAPTER 1
SECRETS IN SPANISH

Leo sprinted to the hallway bathroom, slammed the door, and locked herself in, just in time. An angry knock followed. "Hey, hurry up in there!"

Leo let out a cackle to match her Halloween witch costume. Marisol, Leo's sixteen-year-old sister, banged on the door. She could huff all she wanted; Leo had no plans of letting her in. With four older sisters, Leo was used to these morning races, and it was nice to be on the right side of the locked door for once. Mamá always told Daddy that one bathroom for five girls should be considered cruel and unusual punishment. The house was too small, she said, with only one story and more lawn than living space. Daddy would just wrap his arm around Mamá and say, "You're small too, Elena, but you're perfect for this family."

"Is that you, Leo?" Marisol jiggled the doorknob. "What are you *doing*?"

Leo leaned over the cracked sink, which was always clogged with wads of long dark hair. She dipped a finger in her sour-apple-green face paint, drew along the edge of her forehead, and rubbed down her cheeks.

"Come on, cucaracha," Marisol yelled. She called Leo "cockroach" whenever she wanted to be nasty without getting in trouble for using bad language.

"I'm putting on my costume," Leo shouted.

"Aren't you getting a little too old for costumes?"

"Eleven is not too old." Besides, with Marisol's black leather jackets and ripped tights, she dressed like it was Halloween every day.

Leo wiggled her fingers at the door, the way witches cast spells in movies. *Snakes in your hair,* she thought as loudly as she could, but all she heard was the sound of Marisol sighing against the doorframe. No screams, which meant no snakes, which meant no witch powers. Too bad.

"Marisol," Mamá's voice called out, "leave Leo

alone. Come use my bathroom if you need to."

"My eyeliner is in there," Marisol said, but her footsteps stomped toward Mamá and Daddy's bedroom at the opposite end of the hall.

Another knock came. Softer. "Leo, please hurry," Isabel, Leo's oldest sister, said. "I can help you with your hair if you need me to." Isabel was the only one in the house with the patience to tame Leo's mane of dark curls. Leo's other sisters had inherited shiny smooth hair from Daddy's family, but Leo's hair never went down without a fight.

Checking her reflection one last time, Leo smiled. Her perfect witchy costume was all part of her plan for a perfect Halloween. Now she just had to find Mamá and make her argument. Leo pulled hard on the knob to unstick the creaky door from its frame.

"Boo!" she shouted.

"Thanks, little Leo," Isabel said, not even flinching. "Happy Halloween." She wore a collared shirt and skirt, with only a pair of tiny pumpkin earrings to celebrate the holiday. She slipped into the bathroom, her grown-up heeled shoes clicking against the tile.

Leo couldn't understand why Isabel didn't get more excited. Halloween was one of the best holidays. Not because of the candy or the disguises, even though Leo loved both of those things. No, Halloween was *extra* special because right after it came Leo's *favorite* holiday of all, Día de los Muertos. The thirty-first of October was like Christmas Eve.

For a second, Leo worried that she should have dressed more like Isabel. Would she seem more grown-up without a costume? Then she shook her head, rubbed her green hands together, and set off in search of Mamá.

The hallway filled with morning noises as the Logroño family got ready for the day. Leo shuffled down the hall, her orange-and-black-striped knee socks *shush-shush*ing against the wood floor.

She burst into the kitchen. Sunlight poured through the blinds and onto Mamá's windowsill garden, where the basil and oregano and cilantro glowed bright. Leo might have a green face, but Mamá had the green thumb.

"Mwhahaha," Leo screeched at Daddy, who had his back turned as he sprinkled tortilla bits into the eggs scrambling on the stove.

"Buenos días, Leonora." Daddy smiled at her. "I hope you're hungry." Daddy was good at lots of things, like reading bedtime stories and playing guitar, but he knew how to cook only two things: migas, scrambled egg and tortilla topped with a mountain of cheese; and quesadillas, oozing cheese from each slice. Leo sniffed the air and smiled. Cheesy deliciousness was part of every Logroño breakfast.

Alma and Bélen, Leo's fourteen-year-old twin sisters, rushed into the room with Mamá on their tails. Seeing Alma and Bélen out of bed before 7:30 a.m. was a Halloween miracle, especially since they'd been up late the night before, hogging the bathroom and dying their bangs robin's-egg blue so they could dress as some anime characters Leo didn't know about.

"Has anyone seen my list?" Mamá asked, shooing the blue-haired twins aside.

"What list?" Leo glanced around the cluttered table and shelves. Maybe if she found it, Mamá would see how helpful she could be. Then she'd have to agree to Leo's proposal.

"You mean the list of special—" Belén stopped midsentence when Alma elbowed her.

Leo blinked at her suspicious sisters. "Special what?"

"Oh, nothing." Mamá ruffled a pile of papers on the counter. Leo craned to see.

"Haven't seen it," Daddy answered with his head buried in the frying pan. "Almost time to head out, Leo. Eat up." He divided the migas onto red-and-blue plates with big white Texas lone stars in the middle.

Leo opened her mouth to tell Mamá her idea. The phone rang.

"Hello, Amor y Azúcar Panadería." Mamá answered every phone call with the Spanish name of their bakery, Love and Sugar. Daddy always tried to tell her that she needed to keep the home telephone separate from the business, but there was hardly any point. Everyone in Rose Hill, Texas, knew who to call if you wanted to reach the bakery, and half of them probably had the home phone number memorized.

"Here." Isabel walked into the room, waving a piece of paper.

"Ah, thanks, mija," Mamá whispered, covering the phone mouthpiece. She looked at the paper, then pulled a mechanical pencil out of the tight bun at the back of her head and scribbled something at the bottom. She frowned. "Sí, ya voy," she said, and then spoke Spanish too quickly for Leo to guess the meaning.

Isabel stood close, looking over Mamá's shoulder and nodding. Isabel spoke Spanish. Marisol too. They had both grown up with their abuela singing songs, telling stories, and babysitting them while Mamá went to work. Abuela had been too old to look after babies by the time Alma and Belén were born, but even they were getting better after a year of Spanish classes in school.

Leo, who was too young to have known Abuela and for Spanish class, couldn't speak more than a few words here and there.

Mamá hung up the phone. "Otro hechizo," she said softly. Isabel nodded.

Leo tilted her head and frowned. Mamá only spoke Spanish with customers—or if she didn't want Leo to understand. But that didn't matter now. She had an important goal.

The Diá de los Muertos festival wasn't just the best holiday of the year, or one of Rose Hill's favorite traditions. It was also Amor y Azúcar's biggest event. They sold their cookies and cakes and sweet breads as the whole town celebrated the lives of their ancestors. Mamá's family had hosted the Day of the Dead festival for as long as there had been a Rose Hill, Texas, to celebrate it—or at least that's what Abuela used to say. And getting ready for the festival required a whole day of preparation.

All week Leo had argued for the right to skip school with her older sisters, to get the bakery ready for the festival, with no luck. That was about to change.

"Mamá, I know why you should let me come to the bakery today."

"'Jita, we've talked about this," Mamá said, scribbling on her list without looking up. "I don't want to hear another speech, please." Leo opened her mouth to argue, but Mamá held up a warning finger. "Enough."

"No fair." Leo slammed her fork onto the plate. She felt herself turning whiny, the corners of her mouth drooping.

"Leo, you know it's not a vacation," Isabel said. "Mamá just needs a few extra hands. We're going to be busy all day." She smiled at Leo.

"Leo could help," Belén piped up. The twins were always Leo's best allies. "I mean, just with the normal part—" Alma elbowed her in the side. "Quit it!" Belén snapped.

Marisol tugged Leo's hair from behind. "Mamá and Tía Paloma hog all the baking, anyway, cucaracha. We only get the boring stuff, like taking orders from customers. Believe me, school will be way more fun."

"Mamá," said Leo, turning to her mother, "I love taking orders. I know I can—"

The phone blared again.

"Leo, you will be able to help tomorrow at the

festival," Mamá said as she picked up the call. "Now please go out to the bus stop. Your sisters and I need to leave for the bakery."

Daddy tried to kiss Leo good-bye, but she dodged him, jumping down from the breakfast bar and dumping her eggs in the trash. Anger replaced hunger and growled in her stomach. She stomped out into the foyer. The family cat, Señor Gato, pawed at the front door.

"Do you get to go to the bakery too?" she asked him.

Señor Gato blinked round yellow eyes at her.

"Boo," she hissed at him.

He yawned, arched his back, and trotted into the kitchen with the rest of her family. Leo stomped out the front door alone.

CHAPTER 2
MI AMIGA, CAROLINE

The lower-school bus was empty, as usual. Leo and her sisters had always been the first stop on the route and had their pick of seats. Last year, Leo, Alma, and Belén had sat in a new row every day for their first month of school, which was how Leo knew with absolute certainty that the gray vinyl seat three rows from the back of the right side of the bus had the most cushion left in its foam and the fewest spiderweb cracks in its window.

She pulled her feet up on the seat and reminded herself not to lean her forehead against the glass and ruin her face paint. This far back, she was out of sight of the bus driver, Mrs. Lillis. Totally alone.

The few bites of breakfast she'd eaten sat like a lump in her stomach.

The sky turned bright blue as the bus made its slow, snaking way through Rose Hill. Leo could close her eyes and still see the colorful siding of each house on the route, the well-loved pickup trucks and rusty cars parked along the street, every overgrown lawn or carefully tended flower bed.

But her mind still buzzed with angry thoughts. Mamá should *want* lots of hands in the bakery today. The Day of the Dead festival meant the whole town would come to buy sugar skulls and pan de muerto—bread of the dead, or "dead bread," as Daddy liked to call it. Many people would stop in for bags of bolillo bread or sweet shell-shaped conchas in the weeks following the festival, remembering just how delicious the treats from Amor y Azúcar were.

Mamá always schemed for ways to expand the bakery, make more money, and buy the sprawling two-story house she wanted, right in the center of town. Having a big Day of the Dead festival could help that dream come true. So it made sense that the older girls got out of school to make sure that everything ran smoothly. But Leo was an extra set of hands too.

The bus slowly filled up. Each stop added a couple

of elementary school kids or a large group of middle schoolers. But nobody sat down next to Leo. With Alma and Belén in ninth grade this year, she had no built-in seatmates, and she didn't know how to get new ones. Sisters were so handy for that sort of thing—for sitting next to on the bus, or talking in the courtyard before and after school. Sisters were always hanging around, until suddenly they left you behind.

The bus pulled up to the last stop. Rows filled with kids in masks and sparkling costumes, talking, yelling, teasing, and laughing. Two fifth graders dressed as a lion and a ballerina climbed up the steps and sat in the empty row, right behind Mrs. Lillis's driver's seat. Behind them, a tall blond girl shuffled onto the bus in a dark-purple cloak, holding a glitter-filled magic wand in one hand and a brown paper lunch bag in the other.

Caroline!

Leo waved. "You're back!"

Caroline Campbell slid into the empty spot beside her. Despite the glitter and the rosy cheeks she'd painted on, she looked like a faded ghost wearing a Caroline costume. "I should've called you."

Caroline had been Leo's best friend in third and fourth grade, up until she moved to Houston to be closer to her mom's doctors. The Campbells had moved back to town after Mrs. Campbell died at the beginning of the summer, but Caroline hadn't been in school all year. Leo didn't blame her. She couldn't even imagine what she'd do without Mamá.

"You didn't have to. It's okay." Leo scratched at her tights. When her friend had come back into town, Mamá had sent enough food to feed two Logroño-sized families, and Leo had brought hand-made cards. But mostly, on Isabel's advice, she'd given Caroline some space.

"You picked the best day to come back."

"Brent said I could make an entrance." Caroline flicked her glittery wand in the air.

Leo craned above the seat. "Where is Brent?" Caroline's next-door neighbor was usually the last sixth grader to get on the bus. His backpack was always extra heavy from carrying Caroline's makeup homework to and from school. Leo wouldn't want to be his seat buddy, but he was all right for a boy.

"He's sick. Well, his mom thinks he is, anyway. I am a little bit *dubious*." Caroline half smiled as she used one of Ms. Wood's vocabulary words for the week. She was the kind of person who used the weekly words in real life. "We waited for the bus together, but then he threw up all over his costume.

Now his mom thinks he has the stomach flu. I *told* him not to eat a whole pillowcase of candy yesterday."

Leo laughed. "He didn't really eat that much candy, did he?"

Now Caroline grinned, and Leo finally recognized her friend. "It was a controlled experiment to find out the maximum amount he could eat before throwing up. So tonight he knows exactly when to stop to have the best Halloween ever."

Brent Bayman was the type of person who did controlled experiments in real life.

Leo hugged her stomach and grimaced while she laughed. "What a terrible idea."

"I think he was just trying to make me laugh, you know? I was worried about coming back. . . ."

"Yeah . . ." Leo didn't know what to say, so the silence stretched between them.

"He visited me every day after," Caroline blurted.

Leo's cheeks flushed. Maybe she should've visited more. But Isabel had said not to. And Isabel was usually right about those kinds of things. "I'm sorry I didn't come over—"

"I wanted to be alone. Brent just . . . he lives next door. I couldn't avoid him even when I wanted to." Caroline laughed this time, and Leo smiled.

"I'm really glad you're back."

"Thanks. I think I am too."

The bus turned onto Main Street, just a few blocks from school. "I'm excited I get to be here for the festival this year," Caroline said, pointing at the strings of orange marigolds wrapping the streetlights. "In Houston I would dream about your bakery's cookies. Is everything ready?"

Leo laughed, but it tasted sour. "I guess not. My sisters get to skip school to help Mamá. Everyone's working today except me."

"Really?" Caroline asked. "That's weird."

"I know!" Leo felt a rush of relief to have someone agree with her. "And they acted super weird about it too—speaking Spanish and pretending like it was going to be boring."

"Double weird." Caroline nodded, her face serious. "Um, are you sure that everything's all right?" She spun her bracelet around her wrist.

Leo's stomach lurched, and not just because Mrs. Lillis hit the Main Street pothole too fast. Caroline's parents had whispered and kept secrets before they told her about her mom's cancer, right before they moved to Houston. Leo's family couldn't be keeping a secret like that, could they?

They were almost in front of the bakery now.

Leo leaned forward in her seat to catch sight of the bright blue-and-yellow building that was Amor y Azúcar Panadería. She pressed her face against the window, ignoring the green streaks. The bakery's doors were shut tight, its windows dark.

"Something's wrong."

"What do you mean?" Caroline asked.

"My sisters and mom and aunt are supposed to be working. Mamá had a lot to get ready, and she needed more help to serve the customers and handle the extra baking." Leo repeated the words Mamá had used to shut down her argument all week. "But it's not even open."

Caroline leaned next to Leo and peered out the window too. "Secrets," she said softly.

The bakery slid backward until it slipped out of both their sights.

Leo's heart pounded so hard, she thought it might leap out of her chest. Her mind raced with a thousand possibilities while Caroline chewed on her fingernail.

The bus pulled in front of the school. Everyone rushed out of their seats. Rose Hill Elementary and Rose Hill Middle School shared the same building, and Leo usually felt a surge of superiority when she got off the bus and left behind the K-through-five kids. But today she just felt small and frustrated.

The bell rang. Leo led Caroline toward the sixth-grade classroom, where Ms. Wood, their tall brown-skinned teacher, welcomed Caroline with a packet of rules and a warm smile. Leo helped Caroline settle into the desk next to hers, which had been empty all year waiting for her.

She sat at her desk and doodled in a notebook as the rest of the class shuffled in—goblins and wizards and cats and other witches too, though Leo thought her costume was the best. Later, there would be a parade leading to the gym, where teachers set up booths with Halloween "assignments" like crossword puzzles and ghost-themed math worksheets. Leo usually spent the day collecting candy from the booths with the easiest work and then sitting on the rickety metal bleachers with Alma and Belén, waiting for the costume contest to start. There would be no twins today, though, and Leo wasn't in the mood for crossword puzzles.

A plan started to rise like dough inside Leo.

"Caroline," Leo whispered urgently while Ms. Wood pushed back her fake-nose-and-mustache glasses and continued to take attendance. "Can you do me a favor?"

"What?"

Ms. Wood finished calling roll and put her clip-board on her desk. Leo's fingers twitched.

"My family is up to something, and I have to find out what. I need to get to the bakery and investi-gate. And I thought, since the parade is always so wild, and Ms. Wood won't be counting us once we get to the gym . . ."

Caroline's eyes went wide. "Are you thinking of skipping class?"

"Not class," Leo whispered. "Just the party. I'll probably get caught unless someone covers for me and tells Ms. Wood that they saw me, or that I just went to the bathroom."

Caroline's forehead creased. Leo knew she was asking a lot—it was Caroline's first day back, and a good friend should probably stay to support her. Ms. Wood clapped her hands, and the sixth grad-ers started to line up for the parade. Leo shook her head, stomping down her disappointment. "Never mind," she said. "You don't have to. It was a bad idea anyway."

But Caroline lifted her wand and tapped the top of Leo's black hat. "No, I can do it. Just make sure you line up next to Victoria."

"Huh?" Leo looked around, and then she saw that Victoria Goldman was one of the other wicked witches, with dark frizzy hair hanging over her green face and a pointy black hat. "Oh, smart." Leo slipped into line behind Victoria. It was nice to have Caroline back.

After Ms. Wood led the class out into the hallway, Leo ducked behind the water fountain and then into the bathroom. She stood behind the door of the first stall, listening to her heart pound over the sounds of various classes filing toward the gym.

About ten minutes later, the hallway finally got quiet. Leo ran out of the bathroom, down the hall, and into the street in front of the school, her witch hat clutched to her chest and her shoulders hunched to avoid being spotted.

When she turned the corner safely onto Main, she unhunched her shoulders and looked around. Main Street buildings crowded together, forming a wall of colorful storefronts interrupted only by a parking lot and a gas station at the end of the road near the freeway.

Leo put her hat back on her head and rushed down the sidewalk, past window displays of jack-o'-lanterns and skeletons, hoping no one would notice a little witch with a smudged green face scurrying toward Amor y Azúcar Panadería.

CHAPTER 3
CANDLES, RIBBONS, AND BREAD

On a normal day, Tía Paloma opened the bakery at seven a.m. sharp, after two hours of preparing the kitchen and baking up the first batches of pan dulce. But from two blocks away, Leo could smell that today was different. The air was crisp and cool, with no warm yeasty scent covering the gravel-and-gas smell of the road. When she reached the bakery, its bright wooden door held a chalkboard sign that announced *Please be patient! We're closed today in preparation for Día de los Muertos. Come out tomorrow at nine a.m. for games, traditions, and lots of food!* Underneath that, in smaller letters, the sign added *For special orders and emergencies, just call us!*

Leo stood to one side of the door, so that anyone inside the bakery couldn't see her through the big shelf of colorful skulls and cakes set up in the display window. She heard a car speed down the highway, cheerful pigeons squawking, but not the voices of her family. She tiptoed around to the back of the building and peeked inside the back door to make sure she wasn't about to crash straight into her tía or her mamá. No one was inside.

She pulled the door open. Mamá got on the phone at least once a week to fuss at Tía Paloma about leaving the back door unlocked, but it never did any good.

"Hello?" Leo whispered into the silent bakery. No one answered.

The story about the busy day? It was all a lie.

Leo slammed the door shut and pressed her back against it. She slid down to the ground and buried her green face in her knees. She was so mad her makeup was melting, tears cutting green streaks down her cheeks. Half worried from Caroline's talk about secrets, half furious that she was being left out again, Leo felt her bad feelings swell like cake in an oven. Before she knew it, Leo let out a loud screech, one that would have sent Señor Gato running.

"What was that noise?" someone said.

Leo panicked as she heard voices over the spine-tingling crunch of gravel. She peered out the back window and saw Mamá's muddy maroon car parked in the no longer empty lot. Doors slammed, and Leo's sisters and Mamá piled out.

"Why couldn't I have just gone to school?" she heard Marisol complain.

A lightning bolt of panic zipped through Leo. Mamá would be boiling-oil mad if she found out that Leo had left school without permission. Leo darted away from the door, looking for a place to hide.

She raced past the walk-in refrigerator, where trays of shaped dough, gallons of milk, and crates of eggs waited to be freed from their cling-wrapped stacks. She darted past the long wooden table that took up the center of the kitchen area, spotless and empty, when it was usually covered in piles of flour, hunks of dough, and jars of fruit filling, frosting, and caramel. Leo shot by Mamá and Daddy's empty office, almost crashed into the swinging doors that led to the front of the bakery, and leaned against them to catch her breath when she heard Mamá calling for help emptying the trunk of the car.

She gazed around, looking for a place to hide as the voices in the parking lot grew louder. She backed up and slammed into the cabinets. They stood tall and solid, three of them lined along the walls of the kitchen. Unlike the modern metal ovens or the smooth countertop, the cabinets were carved and cracked, worn down in a way that nothing else in the kitchen was. But right now, as someone struggled with locking and then unlocking the already open back door, the most important thing about the cabinets was that they were big.

Leo pulled open the doors of the first cabinet, crawled onto the bottom shelf between two huge sacks of flour, and shut herself in until only a thin line of light showed where the doors didn't fit together perfectly. She gazed through the crack, able to see half of the bakery kitchen.

High-heeled shoes *click-clack*ed on the orange-brown tiles. Leo tried to lean closer to the crack without making the old shelf creak. She could almost see something—the very edge of a hand and a dark skirt.

"Hello? Yes, I'm here. Where are you?" Mamá wasn't using her customer voice, so it was probably Tía Paloma on the phone, or Daddy. Leo leaned so her ear was pressed against the crack.

"Yes, I have the ribbon. The candles are at your house. No, you took them last time because you said you needed them. I told you we should keep them together, but you said— I'm sure. I'm sure, Palomita. Yes, I— Okay, it's okay. Marisol and I can make them. Just get over here. We're waiting. And don't forget to bring Mamá and Abuelita."

Bring Mamá and Abuelita? Leo shook her head. She must've gotten flour in her ears. Abuela had passed away when Leo was only a toddler, and Mamá's grandmother had been dead for much longer.

Mamá snapped her phone case shut, *click-clack*ed her way to the front of the bakery. Leo heard snippets of her sisters arguing.

Leo thumped back to lean against a flour sack. Her brain felt like a stuffed empanada, with Mamá's words oozing out the sides like guava jelly. Candles? Ribbons? Those were hardly normal baking ingredients. Leo didn't know what her Mamá had planned, but it definitely felt bigger than getting ready for tomorrow's festival.

After a few minutes, she heard noise in the back of the bakery again. The door opened and closed. She leaned forward to take a look through the crack in the cabinet door and spotted Tía Paloma.

"Start the dough, Isa," Mamá said. "We need to set the table."

"Music!" Tía Paloma's high voice rang out. "You're right, Mami, we need music. Elena loves music, and Abuelita, and her abuela. Bisabuela doesn't, but she's an old crab apple anyway."

Who was Tía Paloma talking to? Leo saw Mamá setting one of her woven-plastic shopping bags on the baking table, pulling out candles and cloth and colorful ribbons, and lining them up along the edge of the table. Tía Paloma pushed through the swinging shuttered doors into the storefront, and a few seconds later, a voice moaned what sounded like an old love song in Spanish. Leo thought all songs in Spanish sounded like love songs, because they had so many long wailing notes. They were the kind of songs that made you want to clutch your chest and belt them out as loud as you could.

Leo stopped trying to pick out recognizable words from the crooning music—"amor" was an easy one— and tried to find Isabel. Her sister was measuring ingredients into a small mixing bowl, letting puffs of flour escape to dust the counter as the mixer spun in lazy circles. Leo smelled vanilla, and cinnamon, and something spicy that tickled her nose and comforted her, even though she couldn't decide if it was a familiar smell or a brand-new one.

Tía Paloma came back through the swinging doors and helped Mamá spread a colorful hand-made quilt over the wooden table. Leo recognized the quilt as one of the ones her bisabuela, Mamá's grandmother, had made. Abuela used to make ones just like it, though hers were sometimes sewn out of old T-shirts and clothes that Leo and her sisters had outgrown. Maybe this was what Mamá had meant when she had told Tía Paloma to bring Abuelita?

But still . . . you couldn't make bread on top of your bisabuela's quilt.

The back door slammed; someone sighed in a long huff.

"Your candles." Marisol slammed a bag on the table. Even from her spot in the cabinet, Leo could tell she was rolling her eyes, and Leo rolled her eyes right back. Marisol didn't even care, while Leo would have given anything to be included.

"There you are," Mamá said. "Did it go okay? Are you tired? Why is your phone out? Is that what took you so long?"

Tía Paloma hurried to the back of the kitchen with her arms full of white billowy fabric, then crossed Leo's line of sight again, pushing Alma and Belén through the swinging doors toward the bathrooms in the front of the shop.

"My friends are telling me everything I'm missing at school." Marisol tapped her phone screen.

"Aren't you lucky to be so popular?" Mamá held out a hand. Marisol glowered and dropped her phone into Mamá's palm. "Help your sister with the dough, please. Your friends will fill you in tomorrow."

Marisol sighed and joined Isabel at the counter. Mamá continued to take items out of her bag. When the phone at the front of the store started to ring, Isabel ran to answer it.

"Hello, you've reached Amor y Azúcar Panadería. We're actually closed today, but if you'd like to stop by tomorrow for our Day of the Dead festival, you can." Isabel paused. "Oh! Yes, yes, of course you can. Just give me one minute." She peeked her head into the kitchen, one hand covering the phone. "An order, Mamá," she whispered. "A special order."

Mamá nodded and reached into her pocket, pulling out a folded piece of yellow lined paper and a blue mechanical pencil.

"Two orders of pan de la suerte," Isabel spoke out loud. Mamá scribbled on the paper. "And what's the occasion? Oh, a wedding reception! Yes, we'd be happy to help. If you'll just give me your name and when you need to pick them up . . ." Mamá brought her the paper, and Isabel wrote down the information. "Thank you so much, and have a nice day. Oh, and good luck with the wedding." She laughed.

Pan de la suerte? Leo knew every kind of bread and cake Amor y Azúcar Bakery made, but she had no idea what pan de la suerte was. Didn't "suerte" mean luck?

"Thanks, mija." Mamá took the list back and tucked it into her pocket with the pencil. "We'll have to get more chocolate coins—good thing candy will be on sale after tomorrow. The full moon is on Sunday, isn't it? We'll have to start then. Oh, I can't wait to teach you! I haven't made pan de la suerte in such a long time."

Marisol snorted, but if Mamá heard her, she ignored it. Isabel just smiled. Leo was more confused than ever. She didn't know any kind of bread made out of chocolate coins and moonlight.

Tía Paloma skipped to the long table, where Mamá lined up candles on top of the quilt. Alma and Belén followed, both dragging their feet under long white robes that made them look like angels in a nativity play. The robes tied at the waist with thick red sashes, and the twin's colored bangs were hidden under black veils on their heads. They stood just inside the kitchen doorway, looking almost as confused as Leo felt.

"Oh, who brought a light?" Tía Paloma crooned as she made a last adjustment to one of Mamá's candles. "I meant to, only I got caught up in who knows what and . . ."

Mamá and Marisol reached out from opposite ends of the table—Mamá holding a book of matches, Marisol a purple plastic cigarette lighter.

Leo was grateful that she could only see half of Mamá's face, and therefore only half of the evil eye Mamá aimed at Marisol.

Marisol, though, seemed unaffected. "What?"

"That better not have been in your pocket a minute ago" was all Mamá said.

She snatched the lighter and handed it to Tía Paloma. When Tía lit the first candle, all the lights in the kitchen went out. The radio too stopped playing, and there was no one in the front of the store to turn it off. Leo shivered.

Isabel, Alma, and Belén joined Mamá and Marisol at the table while Tía Paloma continued lighting candles. Isabel dropped a hunk of unbaked dough on the center of the quilt, and all six women spread out until they were spaced evenly around the table.

Before Mamá took her place at one end, her tall frame blocking most of the action from Leo's view,

Leo caught one glimpse of Tía Paloma at the far end with a hand hovering in the air over one of the candles. The flickering flames made colors and shapes strange, but Leo thought for a second that Tía Paloma's eyes had turned completely white, like dollops of wax dripping off the tall white candle in front of her.

The cupboard had always been dark, but now Leo felt the darkness pressing against her. She tried to see what was happening beyond Mamá's back.

"Mujeres," Mamá said, and Leo gripped her knees tighter because Mamá's voice always sounded different when she spoke Spanish, faster and lower and unfamiliar. It was scary to know her Mamá had another voice. "Hijas de nuestra familia, nos unimos juntas aquí para prepararnos, y para dar la bienvenida a nuestras hermanas nuevas, Alma y Belén."

Leo didn't know most of those words, but she knew "familia" meant family (that one was easy), and "hermanas" meant sisters. She thought there were some other words she should have recognized, but it all went so fast that she couldn't pin them down.

A horrible thought popped into Leo's head—did Mamá not want her help because she didn't speak Spanish?

Mamá continued, and Leo could hear the poetry in the words even if she couldn't understand them. She heard the words for bread, and sister and light, and one word that Mamá kept saying that Leo knew she had heard before. It was on the tip of her tongue.

". . . atadas por sangre . . ."

Mamá paused and nodded at Marisol. Leo couldn't see what was happening.

Over the smell of burning candles, the same strange scent that had come out of Isabel's baking slipped through the cupboard crack. Leo wrinkled her nose trying to recognize the tingly smell, but she still couldn't tell if she knew it.

Leo was curious, and she never was very good at ignoring curiosity. If she could just peek around Mamá's shoulder, she would have a view of Marisol and the center of the table. The room seemed dark enough. Leo pushed the cabinet door ajar with a light touch, then leaned out, slowly and so quietly, just far enough that she could see around Mamá's back.

Marisol looked pale and ghostly in the flickering light with her thick black eyeliner. She held out a long silver knife. This was not the sort of knife Mamá kept in the bakery or at home in the kitchen. It was not a butter knife or a steak knife or a knife for chopping vegetables or slicing bread. It was the sort of knife you might see in a movie about elves and knights and princesses and dragons. Instead of a handle, it had what could only be described as a hilt. The bottom of the hilt was a tiny skull decorated with roses and swirling lines.

The cabinet hinge squeaked. Mamá's head tilted at the sound, and Leo pulled her head back in panic. For three long seconds, everything was quiet. Leo waited for footsteps, or for the cabinet door to open.

Instead, Mamá started speaking Spanish again. Leo peeked through the crack, her heart still pounding.

The dough in the center of the table was growing.

Like a soft beige balloon, it expanded to twice its size, then three times, and then kept going until it stretched from one end of the table to the other. The air smelled of flour, cinnamon, vanilla, the mystery smell, and the candles, and Leo even thought she could smell Tía Paloma's funny organic soap and Mamá's perfume. The darkness all around her stopped pressing Leo into a nervous ball. Her shoulders, cramped from hunching over, relaxed; her pulse slowed. She wiggled her toes inside her striped socks and smiled.

Alma giggled, and Belén followed, and Tía

Paloma's high laughter rang out over Isabel's soft chuckle. Even Marisol cracked a smile.

"Shh . . . , " Mamá scolded, but there was a smile in her voice. "Tranquila, girls. And here, take these." She handed Alma and Belén each a cardboard spool of ribbon—pink for Alma, blue for Belén. Marisol, Isabel, and Tía Paloma pulled the sides of the dough balloon so that its top lay flat, and Mamá started speaking Spanish again.

Alma and Belén wrapped their ribbons around and through the dough, weaving them together in a pattern that Leo couldn't see. When the spools emptied, Isabel, Marisol, Tía Paloma, and Mamá reached out and folded the dough in on itself from both sides, and then folded the new corners in and in until the dough was just a bun-sized lump once again. Leo couldn't see the ribbons anymore.

Mamá gave one more speech in Spanish about family, and then, as quickly as they had started, she and Tía Paloma blew out all the candles. The kitchen lights came back on, hurting Leo's eyes with their harsh brightness. The radio moaned about love.

Mamá gathered up the candles into her shopping bag, folded the quilt, and plopped the dough lump straight into the trash can.

"Okay," she said, dusting her hands. "Now that the initiation is all taken care of, start the ovens, please, Palomita. Marisol, your sister will need help filling the conos. Alma, Belén, change quickly so you can start on the pan de muerto glaze. And put your heart into it, please. We have lots of work to do!"

In the bustle that followed, the strange tingly smell slipped away, replaced by the normal bakery smells. Everyone prepared for tomorrow's festival as though nothing unusual had taken place. With the lights back on, Leo was tempted to let the normalness wrap around her like a blanket and shut out her questions.

But one word from Mamá's speech Leo couldn't stop thinking about. The word she hadn't recognized before. "Magia."

Magic.

CHAPTER 4
SUGAR AND STOMPING

Sneaking out of the busy bakery proved much harder than sneaking into the empty one. Leo found her opportunity after two hours scrunched in the cabinet, sneezy and nervous. She darted out the back door while her family crowded in the front of the store to perfect the window display. She snuck back down Main Street and hid in the bushes outside school until she could slip into the bus line.

"Leo!" Caroline found her in their seat at the back of the bus. "What happened? Tell me everything." She scooted into the seat and whispered, "I told Ms. Wood you ate fourteen cookies and had to use the bathroom. She was so busy and stressed out that she just nodded." Caroline's cheeks flushed pink as she held out an orange plastic bag filled with fun-sized candies. "I grabbed some extra for you. Can't go home without candy from the Halloween party."

"Thanks." Leo took the bag. She wanted to tell Caroline what she had seen in the bakery, but she didn't know where to begin. She didn't even know what she had seen. "I didn't get caught by Mamá or my sisters or aunt."

"That's good." Caroline held out a hand for Leo to high five.

Leo's hand stayed limp at her side.

"You okay?"

"Does . . . your family lie to you?"

Caroline didn't answer right away. "My dad tries to be honest, but I think he pretends like everything is okay sometimes. He hides stuff if he thinks it'll be hard for me. Like when . . ." She trailed off.

Leo felt guilty. Her problem wasn't nearly as big as Caroline's mom dying. "It's just . . . I found out something I'm not supposed to know."

Caroline raised her eyebrows, her hazel eyes worried. "You should be honest with them," she said. "They love you." She shrugged, then smiled. "I bet Isabel would know what to do."

Caroline was right. Maybe she should talk to Isabel. Or maybe not. "But they think I'm a baby."

"So tell them you're not a baby."

The bus brakes squealed as they reached the first stop.

"Sorry." Caroline stood up and pulled on her backpack. "I have to go. But you can tell me more about it tomorrow, okay?" One side of her mouth stretched into a smile. "I'll see you at the festival, Leo."

"Bye." Leo watched Caroline exit the bus. Even though it was nice to talk to her friend, she was relieved to stare out the blurry window for the rest of the ride home.

She arrived to a silent house, with a scribbled note from Daddy on the fridge promising to be back soon. "Helping with festival things," the note read.

Festival things. Leo crumpled the note and threw it in the trash. Then she stomped down the hall and into her room, her throat tight. She dropped her backpack on the floor and flopped backward onto the bed, careful of her face paint. She lay with her confused thoughts and grumbling stomach (she had missed lunch), trying to make sense of the bread, the candles, the ribbons, the knife—the magic?

She took the sack of candy that Caroline had

given her and unwrapped every single piece, shoving it into her mouth and eating it without thinking, without tasting any of it—even the Junior Mints. She could feel the stickiness of the chocolate mixing with the dried green paint on her face, and the whole thing made her stomach lurch.

She stood up, her arms and legs full of frustration, and slammed her door so hard it bounced back open. This too annoyed Leo.

"Wow." Marisol poked her head into the room from the hallway. "You're awfully violent today, cucaracha. What happened, the parade got rained out? The costume contest didn't go your way?"

Leo was definitely not scared—not even the tiniest bit—but she was startled when her sister appeared. "What are you doing here?"

Marisol slumped onto the ground by the bed and pulled a bottle of nail polish out of her pocket. "Mamá sent me to check on you." Her smile twisted into a smirk as she coated the nails of her left hand in bright metallic purple. "And to get me out of everyone's hair."

Leo fumed. "I thought the bakery was super busy today."

Marisol blew on her nails and switched hands. "It is. That's why they didn't want me around. Best way to get out of work on a busy day is to break a few spice jars and drop a tray of bolillos."

Leo didn't know if Marisol was joking or not, and she didn't like not knowing. "Marisol," she said, her voice small, "were you really working in the bakery today?"

Marisol finished painting her nails, blew on them, and slipped the bottle back into her pocket. She held out her hands, tilted them back and forth, and then reached into another pocket and produced another bottle, of dark-silver polish.

"Of course. What else would we be doing? What else do we ever do?" She shook and uncapped the bottle and added polka dots to her left-hand nails.

Leo took a deep breath, feeling her frustration pound in her head. "Where do you get all that new makeup from, anyway? You don't even get an allowance."

She wanted Marisol to get mad or embarrassed and yell back. She wanted a good fight. Instead, Marisol closed the nail polish and gave Leo a crooked smile.

"What time do you want to go trick-or-treating? Mamá told me to ask you when she should get home."

Leo didn't care if her family stayed at the bakery all night. "I don't want to go trick-or-treating today," she snapped. "I'm sick." She threw herself onto her bed.

"Too much chocolate today, huh?" Marisol shrugged, tucked the nail polish back into her pocket, and stood up. "Okay, I'll tell her. Feel better, cucaracha. I'll hand out extra candy for you."

Leo's rage faded away as she snuggled under her orange-striped blanket that night. Daddy had brought her ginger ale and Mamá had felt her forehead for a temperature. Isabel had sat next to her and urged her to at least walk up and down the block, and Alma and Belén had tried to tempt her out of bed with handfuls of chocolate. Even Marisol stopped by Leo's room—dressed as an evil queen in silver and purple—to ask if she was feeling better.

But Leo wasn't better. What was everyone hiding? And why was Leo the only one left out?

An angry voice whispered in her head: *You're too little. You wouldn't be serious enough. Besides, you wouldn't understand it, anyway. It was all in Spanish.*

Leo scowled at the wall, at her *Wizard of Oz* poster, and at the imaginary voice. She rolled over in bed so that her other cheek pressed into the pillow. Maybe her family had been doing something religious, like

First Holy Communion. Leo had envied each of her older sisters when they had reached second grade and got to walk with their arms uncrossed to the front of the church every week, eat the communion wafer, and sip the wine. But eventually Leo turned seven and got her very own white dress and party, and there was nothing to be jealous of anymore.

First Communion had never been a secret, though.

Through the tiny window above her dollhouse, Leo could see the moving lights of the interstate beyond the edge of town and the still lights of the stars, flickering like the candles on the bakery table. Leo loved Rose Hill, but she knew it was an in-between sort of place. The cars on the interstate only stopped in her tiny town while zooming from their last place to their next. Rose Hill wasn't important enough, or interesting enough, to compete with Corpus Christi or Austin. Rose Hill might seem perfect to Leo, but in a state as big as Texas, little things got overlooked. Forgotten.

Leo fell asleep staring at the stars.

CHAPTER 5
THE DAY OF THE DEAD

In the morning, the Logroño house spun and hummed like an electric mixer.

"Wake up, Leonora!" Daddy called from the hallway, sing-songing the syllables of Leo's name. "I hope you're feeling better, because I promised your mamá I'd have you all up and out by eight o'clock."

Leo jumped out of bed as the Day of the Dead festival beckoned. It was like waking up on your birthday—tired didn't stand a chance against excited. Even her anger from the night before had vanished with the bright morning sky.

Mamá must have been up early: at the foot of Leo's

bed, her black skeleton T-shirt sat next to her color-ful striped skirt. Leo hopped out of bed, changed out of her pajamas, and skipped toward the bathroom to brush her teeth.

The phone blared, and the bathroom was full.

"Hello?" Daddy answered the phone. "Yes, of course. Leo! Can you grab Mamá's and my aprons from the bedside table? We need to bring them with us."

Mamá and Tía Paloma had been on Main Street for hours already. Leo swished the edges of her skirt, then ran to Mamá and Daddy's bedroom across the hall, where she found the skeleton-decorated aprons not on the bedside table, but hanging over the closet door. She then bounced back to the bathroom, where Marisol and the twins fought for mirror space.

"Will you do my makeup next?" Leo watched Marisol draw a long black smile across her white-painted cheeks. One of Leo's favorite parts of Día de los Muertos was seeing all the colorful skulls on drawings, candy, and faces. As the best artist in the family, Marisol painted Leo's face every year.

"Do it in the kitchen," Belén said. "We've been waiting."

"Hold your horses, all of you," Marisol grumbled. "I got up early on purpose."

"Here, let me braid your hair first." Isabel put a hand on Leo's shoulder and pulled her away from the crowded bathroom.

In the kitchen, Daddy answered another phone call and added a silver serving platter to the table's growing pile of things Mamá needed. Leo added the aprons next to several folded plastic tablecloths and the good muffin tin.

Isabel sat Leo down at the table, grabbed a brush from the counter, and pulled out Leo's ponytail. She smoothed down the frizz at the top of Leo's head. "Are you feeling better today?"

Leo felt energized, her fingers and toes wiggly with purpose. She didn't want to cry or pout anymore. She wanted answers.

"I feel fine," Leo said. "I can't wait to leave already!"

She didn't tell Isabel that what she was most excited for was the chance to search the bakery for clues.

After Isabel dragged the comb through Leo's hair and braided it into pigtails with bright-green ribbons running through them, and after Marisol painted Leo's face into a skeleton mask with curlicues where her smile ended and flowers around her eyes, and after Mamá called five more times, they finally left. Daddy and Isabel sat in the front seats of the old pickup, while Marisol and Leo sat on the tiny cushion seats behind them. The twins—who were the last ones out, after intricately decorating each other's faces in blue and pink face paint—sat in the back of the truck, which Mamá would have hated.

"Are you ready?" Daddy called. "We've got a long drive."

"It wouldn't be so long if you didn't take the scenic route," Alma called back, knocking on the window.

"I'm not driving on the highway with you two back there. Don't worry—if we do a lot of business today, maybe by this time next year we'll be walking to the bakery from our brand-new house. Hold tight, everyone!"

The truck rolled out of the driveway with a grumble and a lurch and a couple of joyous screeches from the twins.

Main Street had looked nice the day before, quiet and decorated, but today it was transformed. It seemed most of Rose Hill was crammed into the two blocks between Amor y Azúcar Bakery and Ms. Flores's taquería, some dressed in elaborate skeleton costumes complete with flowers and ruffled clothing, some in their Halloween costumes, and some in regular clothes. Yesenia Flores, a girl from Marisol's art class, sat outside the restaurant at a table with a long line in front of it, painting skeleton faces onto the kids and adults who had come unprepared. Ms. Flores sold breakfast tacos on the sidewalk, and Daddy bought Leo one of the tinfoil bundles filled with scrambled egg and potato wrapped in a fresh tortilla. Leo could smell tamales cooking inside the restaurant.

Amor y Azúcar had its own outdoor booth, covered with sugar skulls and pastries and paper flowers. Mamá passed out cookies and rolls at the booth in full skeleton face paint, while Tía Paloma worked inside the bakery, serving customers with larger orders. Between the restaurant and the bakery, more stalls offered shiny skeleton trinkets, aguas frescas and other drinks, snacks, and fairground games.

"There are my beautiful girls." Mamá smiled when they reached the booth, her white face paint cracking around her cheeks. "Happy festival, everyone!"

"I'll put some more conchas in the oven." Isabel eyed the empty spaces in the display table. "And maybe more cookies?"

"Thank you, mija." Mamá laughed. "Oh, good, the aprons."

Daddy slipped his over his head, displaying the neon skeleton printed on the front. Mamá put her apron on over her colorful ruffled dress and ran her hands down the front, leaving little streaks of flour. "Perfect," she sighed, kissing Daddy's cheek and reaching to tie the laces around his waist.

Leo helped Mamá and Daddy lift trays while Alma and Belén spread an orange tablecloth over the booth. Music and laughter echoed down the crowded street, and the smell of sweet bread filled her nose. The Día de los Muertos festival had started, and Leo grinned as wide as a sugar skull.

"Marisol, I think Tía Paloma could use help with the customers inside," Mamá suggested. Marisol, her fingers tapping at her phone, walked to the bakery without looking up.

"I'm good with customers!" Leo turned to follow Marisol.

"No, 'jita, stay here a minute," Mamá said. "Alma, Belén, you're running the tent like we talked about. It's over behind the altars. Ask me or Tía Paloma if you have any questions, okay? And tell us if you need a break."

Leo watched her twin sisters nod and poke each

other and giggle like third graders who had just been given hall monitor duty for the first time. For as long as Leo could remember, Tía Paloma had been in charge of the special tent, set up in the back corner of the empty lot in the middle of the block with an old hand-painted banner that simply read *Messages—Mensajes $10.*

Letting Alma and Belén run the tent made no sense. Mamá had always said not to bother Tía Paloma when she worked there, and it should be Mamá or Isabel who took over, not the almost-youngest and giggliest sisters. Leo tugged at a strand of hair that was stuck to her cheek. She felt the sour feeling from last night rise up in her stomach.

"I'll help you." She skipped to catch up with Alma and Belén. But Daddy caught her before she could take more than a few steps, and Mamá shook her head.

"Go enjoy the festival, 'jita. You don't need to spend the day working."

"But I want to help. Alma and Belén are helping." Mamá and Daddy glanced at each other, then busied themselves arranging the table. "Why do *they* get to help?" Leo pressed. "You could tell me how to take the messages and I could do it."

Mamá placed her hand on Leo's forehead. "How are you feeling? I think you'd better take it easy today, 'jita." Mamá raised her eyebrows. "So you don't get sick again."

"But—" *I'm not a baby,* Leo wanted to scream but didn't, because there was no better way to sound like a great big whiny baby.

"Cheer up, Leonora." Daddy poked the corner of Leo's mouth. "Put on a happy face. It's a celebration!"

Stomping away, Leo crashed into the corner of the not-very-sturdy folding table. Mamá gasped as several of the sugarcoated orejas fell to the ground. The ear-shaped pastries were quickly covered in dirt, but Leo didn't turn around. She tossed the uneaten half of her breakfast taco into a plastic trash can and pushed her way through the crowd.

The morning had started off cool and bright, but the clear sky offered little shade, and Leo started to feel drops of sweat drip down her face. Summer in Texas hung around like a stray cat, disappearing for a few days at a time only to show up again when you thought it was gone for good. Leo shuffled past the long table of ofrendas, pretending to admire the altars decorated with flower petals, pictures, candles, and food.

Behind the candles, a hunched woman approached Alma and Belén's tent. Leo craned her neck and recognized one of the old women who used to gossip with Abuela after mass. Leo's curiosity rose.

If no one was going to tell her anything, her only option was to snoop. And she would start with the twins.

Leo ducked and tugged at her shoelace as if tying it, then ran in a crouch behind the table and across the parking lot until she was safely hidden in the back of the tent. A quick peek made sure that no one had watched her run—Leo didn't think that anyone but Mamá would stop her from hanging around the tent, but she didn't want to take any chances, either.

Oddly, a banner was draped along this side too, even though the back of the tent faced a plain brick wall. The banner on the back had no price, but in addition to promising messages, it also read *Welcome—Bienvenidos.*

Strange.

Leo had missed the days of setup this year, but she had been with Daddy last year when all the tables and booths went up. She knew that under the beige plastic canvas of this tent stood a house-shaped skeleton of metal poles, and she knew that the canvas laced together at each corner. Which meant that if she inspected the nearest corner, it would be easy to find a spot where the lacing was loose, where she could peek inside.

Leo peeked.

The visitor was Mrs. Gomez, a short old lady with cropped gray hair and children who had all moved to New York or Chicago or some other big faraway city to be doctors and lawyers. Leo remembered seeing pictures of Mrs. Gomez's youngest daughter when she had gone with Mamá to bring a special box of bread and cookies over after Mr. Gomez had died from a heart attack two summers ago.

Leo leaned to get a view beyond the entrance flap. The space glowed brightly from a skeletal standing lamp that Leo recognized from Tía Paloma's living room. Alma and Belén sat at a little square folding table on one side; next to their table was one of the rolling metal shelves from the bakery, full of pan de muerto. The warm plastic smelled musty, but the inside of the tent made Leo's nose tingle in a familiar way.

Mrs. Gomez walked to the table and sat on the stool Belén nodded at. Leo couldn't see the old woman's face, but she saw the wrinkled hands tremble as Mrs. Gomez fumbled through her purse for her wallet. Alma and Belén smiled encouragingly from their side of the table, but their smiles were less comforting than usual, decorated as they were with skull paint and flowers.

Mrs. Gomez handed Alma a folded bill, and Belén struck a match to light the thick white candle in the center of the table. The lamp went dark, just like the lights in the bakery the day before. Leo struggled to adjust her eyes, but Mrs. Gomez leaned forward on her stool in the flickering light, blocking Alma's face and most of Belén's body except for the arm that reached to the shelf for a piece of bread.

Leo grew tired of looking through cracks and only seeing tiny pieces of what happened. She tugged at the laces of the tent until she had made a big enough hole to stick her head all the way inside, trusting the darkness of the corners to keep her hidden.

Belén put the pan de muerto on the table next to the candle. Belén and Alma shared one of their looks, and after a slight pause, Alma nodded and broke the bread in half, offering one piece to Mrs. Gomez. Belén held her right hand over the flame of the candle and held Alma's hand with her left. The dark made the shadows of their skeletal face paint look like real holes and hollows where their eyes and noses should have been. Even though most of her body was still outside in the sun, Leo shivered.

Alma nodded again. Both she and Mrs. Gomez raised their piece of bread to their mouths. They bit, chewed, swallowed. In the space between Leo's breaths, Alma's eyes turned bright white like two full moons shining out of their dark pits.

"Llama." Belén's fingers still hovered over the candle flame, which danced wildly as though it were being blown by a strong wind.

"Vicente." Mrs. Gomez's voice was soft. "Vicente Gomez."

The flame stopped flickering. The spicy smell grew strong. Alma began to shake.

Belén spoke again, but it wasn't her voice that came out. It was a man's voice, and it came out of Belén's throat. "¿Hortensia? ¿Cómo estás, mi amor?"

Mrs. Gomez's shoulders bounced as she spoke in soft, laughing Spanish, and Belén answered with the deep voice. Alma didn't move, didn't speak, just sat with her eyes shining and her body trembling, looking like a jammed machine.

This was magic. Her sisters were doing magic.

Magia.

Even though she had heard the word yesterday, it sounded out of place in Leo's head. She tested it like a loose tooth: the tent was for practicing magic. The bakery was magic. Leo was seeing—and hearing, and smelling—magic right now.

Leo stared at the back of Mrs. Gomez's pale-blue blazer for a few more seconds, waiting for her thoughts to make any kind of sense. When that didn't work, she pulled her head out of the tent, turned around, and ran as quickly and quietly as she could toward the bakery.

CHAPTER 6
RECIPE BOOKS

Leo ran straight past Mamá and Daddy at their booth and barged through the line of people inside the bakery. Isabel and Tía Paloma bustled behind the front counter, taking orders and swiping credit cards and complimenting guests on their costumes, switching easily between English and Spanish. Marisol leaned in a corner behind the display case, tapping at her phone.

"What's up, cucaracha? Why aren't you playing with your friends?"

Leo stomped past her sister, barely hearing the question over her own racing heart.

"Mamá said I could help," Leo lied to Isabel. "If you're busy here, I can help take trays out of the oven."

"Leo." Isabel tried to frown without dropping her salesperson smile.

"I want to help," Leo repeated with a stubborn frown.

Isabel kept smiling. "It's nice of you, Leo, but you don't need to worry about business. You should be outside having fun."

"Fine." Leo puffed out her chest. "Then I guess I'll just go see if Alma and Belén need anything."

Just as she'd hoped, Isabel and Tía Paloma stopped, frozen. "Don't do that," Tía Paloma blurted, at the same time as Isabel said, "You can take trays out if you want."

Leo nodded and stomped past her aunt and sister, ignoring the guilty twinge in her stomach. She marched through the swinging doors into the back of the bakery, and nobody stopped her. *Perfect.*

Isabel and Tía Paloma had set up row after row of trays ready for baking in a line across the counter, and the timer on the oven showed that Leo had ten more minutes before this batch of cookies was done. The preparation would make it simple for Isabel or Tía Paloma to switch trays in and out of the oven—they really didn't need Leo's help. They never did.

Leo spun in a slow circle, inspecting the red-brown tile floor, the sunny yellow walls, and even the bumpy white ceiling for anything suspicious, anything that would explain what she had seen at the bakery yesterday or in the tent just now. She checked under the counters and inside all the drawers. She ran her hand over every inch of the big wooden table, looking for carvings or secret compartments. Her inspection turned up nothing but a few wads of gum that someone (Marisol) had stuck under various surfaces.

She tried the walk-in next. It was too cold to spend much time in the refrigerated pantry, and Leo was always afraid of the heavy metal door slamming on her and trapping her inside, but she poked her head into the cold room and looked around for anything suspicious. Unless magic users needed egg cartons and jugs of milk, she saw nothing.

What sorts of things *would* they need? What kind of magic was going on in that tent? Leo recalled Alma's white eyes, Belén's croaking voice. She had seen part of a movie about a possessed girl once, before Mamá caught her and sent her off to bed. Were Alma and Belén possessed?

Leo let the walk-in door creak shut and faced the kitchen again. This time she turned to the big cabinets on either side of the room. She started with the left side, the one she had hidden in and the ones that held the most common kitchen supplies. It didn't take her long to inspect the bags of flour, spatulas and whisks and spoons, waxed paper, and jars of fruit filling.

The cabinets on the right side of the room were used less frequently, but when Leo pulled open the door of the first cabinet, the contents of its shelves were disappointingly ordinary, though more cluttered than the other cabinets. Leo saw some of the less-common baking supplies, like cloves for the Christmas specials, and macadamia nuts. One shelf held extra office supplies and one whole cabinet carried all the holiday decorations, minus the ones that were up around the bakery now. Leo's heart pounded when she found a bag of chocolate coins next to a bundle of dried plants she didn't recognize and a collection of half-burned candles in all shapes and sizes, but those hardly counted as proof.

What was she looking for, anyway? She'd spent hours watching Mamá and Tía Paloma in the bakery mixing dough, shaping pastries, and arguing about prices and ways to attract new customers. She had chased Alma and Belén around every counter and corner and had found all the best places to hide when Marisol needed someone to fight with. If there were any dark passageways to underground caves or secret cauldrons full of bubbling potions, Leo would know about them already.

But she had seen the candles, the knife, and the dough.

Even now, staring at the burned candles and tinfoil coins, she felt it like the way you can feel a thunderstorm before it happens. Her family *was* keeping secrets, big ones, and there had to be proof of it somewhere.

There was one place where Leo wasn't allowed to run, explore, or poke around: the office. Past the walk-in, the door to the bakery office was cracked open, an invitation Leo couldn't resist. The closetlike space was crowded with two desks, two mismatched filing cabinets, and an ancient computer that Mamá never stopped complaining about. Shelves high out of Leo's reach held binders that were labeled by year and that strained to contain too many papers and receipts. Half hidden behind the door stood the shelf of cookbooks, magazines, and index cards with recipes for everything the bakery had ever made or ever imagined making.

Leo checked all the drawers, flipped through the piles of stacked paper, and even pushed the rolling chairs aside to examine the space under each desk. She found a lot of boring numbers on a lot of boring papers, and she found pens, pencils, paper clips, and rubber bands. Not a single thing caught her eye until she knelt to read the titles of the cookbooks on the bottom shelf.

One book leaned diagonally to fit the shelf, tall and thick with a cover of faded red leather. As soon as she saw it peeking out of its dark corner, Leo had to touch it. The spine was cracked and blank, and there was no title on the front cover, but Leo carefully pulled the book into her lap and opened to the first dusty page, where she read in what looked like handwritten cursive:

Recetas de amor, azúcar, y magia.

Recipes. Leo made what her teacher would call an educated guess. *Recipes of Love, Sugar, and Magic.* The back of her neck prickled.

Leo pushed the office door closed with her back so that she was better hidden from the rest of the kitchen. The bakery was busy, and the timer on the ovens hadn't gone off yet. The prickling spread down to her fingers and toes. This was what she had been looking for. She turned the page.

The first recipe in the book included an inky

black-and-white drawing of round rolls topped with doughy Xs to indicate crossed bones, the same rolls that Alma and Belén were selling in their tent.

PAN DE MUERTO MENSAJERO
PARA HABLAR CON LOS ANTEPASADOS

INGREDIENTES

¼ taza de azúcar

1 cucharadita de levadura

½ cucharadita de sal

2 cucharaditas de semillas de anís

1 cucharadita de canela

2 cucharaditas de hueso en polvo

3 tazas harina

¼ taza de leche

¼ taza de mantequilla

¼ taza de agua

2 huevos

1 cucharadita de ralladura de naranja

2 gotas de tinta

PREPARACIÓN

Combina los ingredientes secos en un tazón, menos 1½ tazas de harina. Calienta la leche, la mantequilla, y el agua en una cacerola, y agrega las gotas de tinta cuando la mezcla está hirviendo. Pon la mezcla de leche en el tazón, y agrega los huevos. Mezcla con ½ taza de harina, y agrega más harina lentamente mientras recitas los nombres de tus seres queridos muertos, hasta que la masa se ponga suave y un poco pegajosa.

Amasa por diez minutos. Debe tener una consistencia suave y elástica. Déjala reposar en un tazón cubierto por dos horas. Haz formas de huesos con la masa, para poner encima del pan. Hornea durante de 45 minutos.

"Para hablar con los antepasados," Leo read aloud. To talk with . . . someone. The recipe called mostly for the things she expected: flour, milk, butter, water, sugar, eggs, and salt, and she knew that bread of the dead usually included anise and cinnamon and orange flavoring, but Leo stared for a long time at the word "hueso," which she thought meant bone.

The next page had the title *Tartas de la verdad— para obtener respuestas verdaderas.* The picture showed a woman standing over another woman in a chair, leaning over her and pointing a finger as if she was demanding la verdad, the truth.

Pastel para pelo showed tufts of hair sprouting

from a bald head, while *Azúcar de la amistad* showed two women hugging over cups of tea. Leo turned the page and found *Pan de la suerte*, with instructions that included the words "luna," "chocolate," and "oro." The words stood under a picture of a white rooster, like the statue Mamá had on her bedside table that was supposed to bring good luck.

Leo leaned closer to the page, close enough to smell the dusty paper and the hint of that now-familiar spicy scent. It was the smell of her family and their secrets. The smell of magic.

"Leo? Where did you go? Didn't you hear the timer beeping? Leo?"

Leo wanted to move, to shove the book back onto the shelf or cover it with one of the other cookbooks, but she couldn't act fast enough. Isabel was already pushing open the office door. She found Leo sitting with the book in her lap, the drawers of the filing cabinets and desks still wide open.

Leo looked at Isabel. Isabel looked at Leo. Although she felt frozen in place, Leo's mind flashed through several thoughts:

Mamá would be furious if she found out. Which meant that . . .

Mamá couldn't find out. And so . . .

Leo needed Isabel on her side.

Leo wasn't sure if she was faking or not, but it was easy to call tears to her eyes. "I'm sorry!" she cried out before Isabel could do anything but stare, mouth open, at the recipe book. "I didn't mean to sneak around, but no one tells me anything. Pleeeease, Isabel, don't tell Mamá. I just want to know what's going on."

"Leo." Isabel sighed, her eyes turning as soft as melted chocolate chips. "Sweetie, put that away. You don't need to worry about it right now."

"You have to tell me." Leo didn't bother to keep the whine out of her voice. "It's not fair!"

"I know, but if you just wait a couple of years . . ."

Leo sniffled, trying to keep her tears from spilling over onto her face paint.

"Isabel?" Marisol's voice droned from the front. "Where'd you go?"

Isabel threw up her hands, pursed her mouth, and spun around. Her heels *click-clack*ed as she walked to the front of the bakery. "I have a special customer on the phone. Will you be okay here for a few minutes?"

"I didn't hear the phone—" Marisol started; then her voice cut off. Isabel must be giving her best Mamá glare. "Sure, whatever. We can manage."

"Thank you."

Isabel *click-clack*ed back to the office, looked around, shut the door, and handed Leo half of a large sugar cookie. She started closing drawers and straightening the desks.

"Okay, little Leo, I'm not promising anything, but if you want me to keep your secret, you have to tell me what you know so far."

CHAPTER 7
FLOUR SNOWFLAKES

Leo took a huge bite of the cookie and ticked the points off on her fingers as she chewed. "The bakery is magic," she said, trying to look sure and determined and not let her voice drift up into a question. "Alma and Belén and Marisol and you and"—she paused for another bite of cookie—"and Mamá and Tía Paloma are all magic. The twins are doing something scary in the messages tent. That book had magic recipes for luck and growing hair." Leo thought about the past few days to see if she was missing anything. "Oh, and magic smells kind of like cinnamon, or cloves, but better and more spicy."

Isabel sat down in Mamá's rolling chair. She rubbed her forehead with her thumbs. "Did you know you've been snooping since before you could talk? I used to catch you crawling into the cabinets at home and pulling out all the pots and pans."

Leo tried to look very surprised, as though crawling into cabinets was something she had done a long time ago instead of something she had done just yesterday.

"You were always asking questions, too," Isabel continued, "and you wanted to do everything we all did. Remember you cried because Mamá wouldn't let you go to school when Alma and Belén did?"

Leo remembered that story, even if she couldn't remember it actually happening. It wasn't hard to imagine her four-year-old self feeling like her older sisters had left her behind.

"Mamá would be so upset if she knew about this," Isabel said. "You're still so little, and these things can be dangerous, Leo."

"I am not little." Leo stuck her chin out and frowned. "I'm eleven and a half, and that's big enough for everyone to stop treating me like a baby!"

Isabel slowly shook her head. "Mamá is going to kill me. . . ."

Leo felt her stomach twist into nervous knots

as Isabel stared down at her. Isabel, who hated to make Mamá mad. Isabel, who was so proud of the responsibility Mamá and Daddy gave her.

It took one very long minute before Isabel smiled the same smile she used when she was offering to comb Leo's hair. "Oh, don't look so sick. I'm not a tattletale, no matter what you and Marisol think. But no more snooping, Leo. Enough."

Leo hung her head. "But . . ."

"What?" Isabel looked down, straight into Leo's best puppy-dog face. "Oh, Leo, no . . . you already figured too much out. I can't tell you any more."

Leo let her bottom lip poke out, hoping that Isabel could be convinced. "Please," she said, "everyone's lying to me. I just want to know the truth."

"I really can't . . . Mamá . . ." Isabel tugged on her earring, a sure sign that she was about to give in.

"I'm responsible," Leo blurted. "Um, at least I can be more responsible. And I can learn Spanish. I can fix whatever I need to fix."

"Leo," Isabel looked ready to cry, "it isn't something you did wrong. It's just . . . we have a rule . . . Mamá would be . . . Oh, all right!" Isabel cracked. "I guess I can tell you. It can't do any more damage, right?" She sighed, but a smile crept onto her face and she patted Leo's shoulder. "Give me the book, little Leo, and I'll show you something fun."

Leo handed the book over and moved off the floor and into Daddy's desk chair next to Isabel.

"The women in Mamá's family have always been brujas."

"Brujas?" Leo didn't know the word.

"'Bruja' means witch." Isabel pulled off small pieces of her cookie half and began popping them into her mouth. "But we're not just any kind of witch. Brujería is practiced by lots of people in lots of different ways, and our special family power comes from the magic of sweetness; sweetness from love and sweetness from sugar. That's why Mamá's bisabuela started the bakery—she wanted to share love and sugar with everyone, with or without magic." Isabel traced her finger over the spine of the recipe book. "She wrote down all her spells in this book, so that her daughters could follow them. Although . . ." Isabel shrugged. "We don't use the book so much anymore. Mamá set me and Marisol to work typing some of them up on the computer. But every new spell that someone invents gets written down here, to make it official. Any woman in the family can add new recipes."

Leo felt a rush of pride. She wanted to hold the book again and touch the words written by her great-great-grandmother, by her grandmother, maybe even by Mamá.

"Can I do magic too?" she asked. "I haven't done any yet, I don't think. Should I have done any yet? Do I have to make bread with ribbons?"

"Leo, slow down." Isabel frowned. "You have the ability to do magic—we all do—but it's normal that you haven't noticed it yet. The signs don't show until you're older, and it takes practice."

Leo stifled a groan. Everything always hinged on being older. "What signs?"

Isabel shook her head. "Go grab one of the small bags of flour and bring it here, will you?"

Isabel flipped to a page near the back of the book. Leo had one hundred million and seven questions that absolutely could not wait, but she suspected that the very top one on the list—*Can I see some magic?*—would be answered if she listened to Isabel, so she ran out of the office, pulled open the cupboard, and returned with a paper sack of all-purpose flour, one pound. She was finally getting an explanation, and Isabel had done something Mamá didn't want her to. In this moment, anything might be possible.

"Thanks, little Leo." Isabel kept smiling. "Now, this was the first spell I added to the book. It's—it's sort of silly, but I've always liked the small details, the decorations and frostings . . . you know."

Leo nodded. She knew that Isabel loved to use the icing bags to pipe flowers around the edges of tres leches cake and write *¡Feliz Cumpleaños!* or *Felicidades* in fancy script. She also knew that Isabel didn't really think that this spell—whatever it was—was silly. It was special, precious, and Leo felt all the sweetness of her sister's love in the offer to share it. She leaned over the book and read along with Isabel: *Nieve de harina.*

"Snow?" Leo asked.

"Flour snow," Isabel translated. "Flour snowflakes, really. You'll see." She opened the bag of flour. She took a pinch of the white dust with her right hand and placed it in the palm of her left hand.

"Baking and magic have the same three parts," she explained. "One: the ingredients. Always make sure your ingredients are the best you can get, so that your spells and your cakes are as strong and fresh and rich as possible. Two: the recipe or spell. The what and how and when and at what temperature—the more complicated the recipe, the more carefully you have to follow it. Three: the heart. You know you have to put your heart into baking, right? It's the same with magic."

Leo nodded, her heart knocking against her chest.

Isabel's words didn't feel like strange magic; they were familiar advice. Mamá always encouraged her daughters to put their own spin on recipes, to trust their taste buds, and to add love to every mix. "It's a recipe, not a rule book," she had said once when Isabel was worrying over substituting brown sugar for white. Leo felt warmth spread from her stomach to her cheeks as excitement filled her. Isabel's explanation felt like a perfectly solved math problem—Leo didn't need to check her work to know that it made sense.

"This spell is easy in one way," Isabel told Leo, "because it's almost all heart. That means it's good practice for tapping into your power, but it also means you can't rely on the power of the recipe or the ingredients to create the magic for you. It's good for beginners." Isabel blew gently on the palm of her hand and sent the flour flying into the air. The powder clumped and grew, molding itself unnaturally until the air in front of Leo's face was a flurry of flour snowflakes drifting lazily toward the ground, where they puffed back into normal dusty flour piles.

Leo laughed and stuck out her tongue to catch one of the snowflakes, which tasted almost like a gingersnap. "It's magic," she said. "That spicy smell.

That taste. It's the magic, isn't it?"

Isabel nodded, smiling. Goose bumps prickled up Leo's arms. This was magic, and Leo wanted *more*.

When all the snowflakes had puffed away, Isabel dusted off her hands and started to roll the bag of flour closed.

"Wait!" Leo threw up her hands, desperate not to let Isabel return to her normal rule-following self just yet. "You have to let me do it, Isabel. Can I do it? You have to teach me."

Isabel hesitated, her hands frozen on the flour. "I don't know if that's a good idea."

"Isabel," Leo begged, "please. It's just a tiny spell, and I just want to see if I can do it. I just want to see if I really have magic."

"It's not a question of whether you have magic, Leo." Isabel sighed. "It's that you aren't ready to use it yet." But her hands on the neck of the flour bag didn't move. Leo waited.

"Okay," Isabel said after a long pause. "Here's the deal. I know how exciting the magic can be, and I hate when Mamá makes me wait to learn new things, and I don't want to do that to you. But if I trust you, you have to promise to use your good judgment, okay?"

Leo nodded so hard her neck popped.

Isabel sighed. "Mamá is going to kill me," she said again. "But what am I supposed to do? Say no to that pitiful face?" She unrolled the bag, reached in for a pinch of flour, and placed it in Leo's outstretched palm. "I hope you appreciate how much we spoil you, baby of the family."

"I do," Leo said.

"You can try the spell, but don't be disappointed if you don't get it on your first try. You're still young, and it's hard to learn how to get hold of the magic. It takes patience."

Patience had never been Leo's strong point. She immediately blew on her palm and coughed as the flour rose in a cloud and choked her. Isabel covered her mouth, but her eyes betrayed her amusement. Leo frowned.

"Why can't I do it?" she asked, her voice small. A louder voice inside her head, the voice that whispered mean things about her hair and convinced her to stay quiet around strangers, spoke up: *You probably don't have magic.* Maybe every woman in Mamá's family carried magic powers *except* for Leo. "What's wrong with me?"

"Absolutely nothing," Isabel explained. "Except that you're eleven. We start training at fifteen. That's when Mamá will tell you all the history, and you'll be initiated into the family magic, and—"

"Like Alma and Belén!" Leo interrupted. "With the candles and the dresses and the dough. But they're only fourteen still."

"Leonora, how do you know about that?" Isabel looked shocked, and Leo shoved the last bit of her cookie into her mouth to hide her guilt. "No." Isabel shook her head. "Please don't answer, actually. I'm sure I don't want to know. Yes, we initiated Alma and Belén a bit early. It's just that Tía Paloma tires out so quickly, and Mamá didn't want to force her to run the tent by herself for another year. . . ."

"The tent for talking to dead people." Leo took another pinch of flour and blew on her hand again, trying to imagine adding the spicy cinnamon smell to her breath. No snowflakes.

Isabel nodded. "Messages," she said. "Just short ones, usually. The twins have the power to channel the dead, but it drains them. They're lucky to share the gift."

Leo nodded, her heart pounding. Her sisters were possessed, but not by evil spirits like the movie. They were possessed by dead people, by Mrs. Gomez's dead husband, by any other visitor from the other side. It sounded scary. But, Leo thought, Day of the Dead was invented as a way to talk to people who have passed away, to remember them and show them that you still loved them. If messages helped people do that, they couldn't be so scary.

Leo looked at the flour she had spilled on the floor, disenchanted. She bit her lower lip and tried not to show her disappointment. "Why—"

"Don't worry," Isabel said softly. "I told you, no one gets a spell right on their first try, especially before they turn fifteen." She cupped her hand over Leo's, hiding the flour. "Just forget about the magic for now, and you can try again in a few years. At least now you know, right?"

Leo shrugged. She didn't want to wait until she was fifteen. If Alma and Belén could be initiated early, then she could be too. She would just have to prove to Mamá how talented she was, and how much help she could be.

"Can I see you do it?" Leo asked. "Just one more time?"

Isabel smiled, waved toward the dusting of flour on the ground, and held out her cupped hands to catch the resulting storm of snowflakes. They danced upward through the air like someone had hit rewind on winter. When it was finished, the floor was clean and Isabel held a bit of flour, which she carefully brushed into the trash can under the desk.

"You did it different!" How could she learn if her sister was going to change the rules from moment to moment? "You didn't blow on it."

"I told you—this spell isn't about having a strict recipe." Isabel laughed. "It's about the feeling. Don't worry; you'll understand someday."

Leo frowned and reached for one more pinch of flour. "Someday" didn't interest her. She had tried thinking about magic, scrunching her forehead and puffing her chest, as if she had some previously undiscovered magic muscle she could flex. Now, instead, she focused on the flour in her palm and thought about snow.

Leo had seen snow only once, four Christmases ago when Rose Hill had suffered through an unusually cold winter. On Christmas Eve, after Mamá had bundled Leo into her warmest red jacket and piled everyone into her minivan for midnight mass, Leo sat in the pew snug between Daddy and Mamá and fell asleep to the voices of her family and neighbors singing verses of "Silent Night" in English, Spanish, and German. She barely stirred when Daddy carried her out to the truck, or when he tucked her into the seat between Isabel and Marisol. But on the way home, Isabel shook Leo's shoulder and Alma and Belén and even Marisol *ooh*ed and *aah*ed because the freezing night had really frozen, and small white dots sprinkled the windshield.

When they pulled into the driveway, everyone got out of the car and stood in the front yard, heads tilted, arms outstretched. Mamá called it un milagro—a Christmas miracle. Daddy scooped up the thin layer of snow that was sticking on the roof of his truck and made a snowball that hit Mamá when Marisol ducked. Alma and Belén crouched to watch the snowflakes melt as they hit the sidewalk. Isabel hummed Christmas carols and smiled and waved at the neighbors, who were also outside, some in robes and slippers, some still in church dresses and ties. And Leo stared up at the sky and watched the flakes dance like lazy shooting stars.

It was a sweet memory and a snowy memory, and Leo held on to it as she closed her eyes and blew on the flour in her palm. Her breath felt cold against her skin. She opened her eyes and breathed in the smell of flour dust and the tiniest hint of spicy magic.

"Oh, Leo, that's wonderful." Isabel clapped her hands as the small snowstorm whirled and disappeared. "See? You have nothing to worry about. In a few years you'll start training with Mamá and you'll learn to use recipe spells and—oh!" Isabel pulled Leo into a hug. "You're growing up so fast, little Leo. Go enjoy the festival now, won't you? The magic will wait. Besides, I have work to do."

Leo nodded, her throat suddenly tight. "Thank you," she whispered. "Thanks, Isabel."

"What are big sisters for?" Isabel stood, wiped her hand over Mamá's desk to make sure no flour was left on it, and put the spell book back on the shelf where Leo had found it. "But Leo, try to be patient, now. Remember, best judgment." She rolled the top of the flour bag closed and took it with her back into the kitchen and out through the blue swinging doors to the front of the bakery.

With the rule-breaking Isabel fading away, Leo knew she had to act now if she wanted to learn more about magic. She loved her sister, but she couldn't stop after one puny snowflake spell. Moving fast to avoid suspicion, Leo darted to the bookshelf and pulled out the biggest hardcover cookbook she could find. *Make Cakes Like the Greats!* She pulled the glossy paper dust jacket off the book and wrapped it over the spell book. It wasn't a perfect fit, but Leo thought that if she tucked the book under her arm, no one would notice the creases. She peeked out from between the blue doors, made sure to wait until Isabel had her head buried in the display case reaching for a special pink cookie, and then ran. Out from behind the counter, through the line of people, out the front door, and into the bustling street.

Mr. García played his guitar for a small audience and sang requests for old songs and love songs and songs for the dead. Mamá and Daddy sang along as they passed out thin sample slices of pan dulce to anyone who walked by their table. Leo squeezed the magic book between her elbow and her ribs, hoping her skull face paint masked her guilty nervousness.

"Can I have the keys?" she asked Daddy when his hands were full making change. "I want to leave my book in the car."

Without even looking up, Daddy pulled the truck keys out of his apron pocket and dropped them onto the table. "Go play some games, mija," he said while smiling at a customer.

Leo nodded, grabbed the keys, and walked away as fast as she could without looking too suspicious. She left the book of spells in the cab of Daddy's truck, tucked under the backseat so no one could look in and see it.

Only then did she return to the festival and go looking for Caroline.

CHAPTER 8
BREAD AND ALTARS

Leo raced around the festival trying to track down her friend. She wandered down the block, passing a ring-toss game and the aguas frescas stall. She zipped past papier-mâché skeletons and masks and dodged a group of teenagers throwing sugar skulls at each other.

She searched for Caroline's ponytail and finally caught sight of her friend standing next to her dad by the breakfast tacos.

"Caroline!" Leo called.

"Leo, hi!" Caroline smiled hugely, waved with a colored paper skeleton, and left her dad to meet Leo across the street. She wore a crown of yellow-orange paper flowers, but her face was unpainted and her T-shirt was plain green. "Wow," she said. "Love the face paint."

"Thanks. Have you tried any of my mom's pan dulce?"

"Not yet. My dad and I just got here."

"But I have eaten three." Brent Bayman appeared behind Caroline and stepped right into their conversation. In one hand he held one of the bakery's plastic bags, and with the other he stuffed half a pan de muerto into his mouth.

Caroline rolled her eyes and laughed.

"Hey," he said with a nod at Leo. His throat bulged as he swallowed, and then he smiled. "These things are really good." The second half of the pan de muerto disappeared into his mouth. "*Rully* goo," he repeated, spraying crumbs across the sidewalk.

"Excuse *you*." Caroline looked down at her friend and shook her head. "No manners," she whispered to Leo, grinning.

"I got you one." Brent held out the bag to Caroline. "Sorry, Leo, I didn't get you any. But you can get them for free, probably, right?" He watched with hungry eyes as Caroline ripped off a small bite of her roll and then a bigger chunk. Finally Caroline broke off a chunk and offered it to him, rolling her eyes. "You are a bottomless pit."

"Actually, I am a pit capable of consuming almost two pounds of candy before I overflow," Brent corrected her. "I haven't yet tested my limit of sweet bread, but it's less dense than candy, so I bet I could get three pounds in before throwing up."

Leo giggled. "Gross."

"It's not my fault I like it so much," Brent complained. "We never have bread in my house. My little sister's allergic to gluten."

"But you come over and eat all the bread at my house!" Caroline laughed.

"You know," Leo said to Brent, "I bet if you went and told my tía that I sent you, she'd give you a free sample of anything you want in the bakery."

"Really?" Brent's eyes widened. "What are we waiting for?"

"Go ahead," Caroline said. "I want to show Leo the altar."

"Later." Brent didn't hesitate before hurrying back toward the bakery.

"What is the matter with boys?" Caroline asked as she pulled Leo toward the ofrenda table in front of Alma and Belén's tent. It was filled up with mini altars placed by families in memory of loved ones.

Orange marigolds and white candles spread across the tables, and colorful strings of papel picado— tissue paper cut into intricate designs—lined the edges. Some people had set up beautiful multilevel shrines complete with glossy portraits of the dead, bottles of Coke or alcohol, painted skeletons, and pan de muerto rolls. Families who had spent less time preparing for the holiday clumsily assembled altars with the help of construction paper and craft supplies strewn across the tables, laughing at their lopsided results.

That was the part Leo loved most about the festival: everyone got to celebrate in whatever way they wanted, and nobody was left out—even if they didn't know what they were doing.

"This one is ours," Caroline said, pointing to a construction-paper altar near the end of the table. "We made it first thing when we got here." The altar stood up folded in three parts like a poster board, with a picture of Mrs. Campbell, a bottle of orange Fanta, and a decorative marker pattern of butterflies and flowers. "It's not very good." Caroline blushed.

"It's perfect," Leo said, her heart hurting. She wanted to tell Caroline about the secrets, the magic, the messages. The twins' tent was so close—it wouldn't be fair not to tell Caroline that there was a way to speak to her mother again.

"I thought I would be sad," Caroline admitted quietly. She touched the altar. "I've always loved the festival, but . . . I thought it would be too hard this year. I thought it would remind me how much I miss her. But it's a celebration, and I feel good."

Leo closed her mouth and bit her lips closed. Maybe telling Caroline about the magic wasn't such a good idea right now. What if she didn't believe, or thought Leo was making fun of her? What if she was just starting to feel better, and talking to her mom made her sad again? Besides, Leo didn't want to let her family down, spreading their secret right after Isabel had trusted her with it. Instead of speaking, Leo hugged her friend.

"So," Caroline said after a minute, "are you going to tell me about skipping class?"

Luckily for Leo, she didn't have to make up a lie, because Brent returned with two fistfuls of sweet bread. Caroline gave Leo a wink and mouthed, "Tell me later," but Leo only glanced guiltily back at the bakery. She didn't want to break Isabel's trust, or do anything to hurt Mamá. What was worse— breaking her promise to her family, or keeping secrets from her best friend?

CHAPTER 9
NAUGHTY COOKIES

The festival lasted late into the night, with candles and songs and a parade of people walking from Main Street to the graveyard on Azalea Drive to honor their departed loved ones with more offerings, music, and flowers. After the streets cleared, Tía Paloma and Isabel closed down the bakery while Mamá, Daddy, and the exhausted twins helped the other volunteers pack away the tables and tents and chairs that had been set out. Marisol hid behind the counter, texting her friends, and Leo stood nervously in the bakery kitchen, making sure no one went into the office to discover the book was missing.

Leo apologized for knocking the cookies over earlier. Mamá couldn't stop smiling, patting Leo on the head and kissing Daddy's cheek and dreaming out loud about the mansion she could buy if every day had this much business. With all the orders taken, their dream house was getting closer every day. By the time Daddy drove the truck home, the family barely had energy to wash the paint off their faces before falling asleep, and in less than an hour the house was silent.

But Leo couldn't sleep. With the moon shining through her window blinds, Leo stared at the door to her closet, where she had hidden the stolen recipe book. Tires screeched on the highway, and the floating red numbers on Leo's alarm clock showed midnight. Leo pushed aside her comforter and tiptoed across the room, dodging coloring books and dolls left all over the floor. She groped through her underwear drawer for the hidden book. The house stayed silent. Leo pulled the chain on her bedside table lamp and flipped the pages, inhaling the paper-and-bread scent.

She wanted to do more magic. She *had* to do more magic. Her hands and legs itched and her brain whizzed.

Leo's bedroom was the smallest in the house,

but that had never bothered her much because her room came with perks. The entire back wall was lined with built-in bookshelves surrounding a long desk that held the red-and-white wooden dollhouse Daddy had built for Isabel and Marisol, that had been passed down to Alma and Belén and finally to Leo. Now Leo pushed aside Oso the teddy bear and Susan Marie the rag doll, spread the recipe book open across the desk, and climbed onto her bedside table to reach the top shelf, where Mamá and Daddy stored all the boring grown-up books that didn't fit in the living room.

Leo stretched up until she could reach the English-Spanish dictionary Alma and Belén had shared for their eighth-grade Spanish class. She placed the thick blue paperback next to the leather-bound spell book and pulled her old rocking horse over so she could sit facing the desk. She opened the recipe book and started flipping, paying attention mostly to the illustrations and any words she recognized.

Some recipes took up multiple pages and seemed to require weeks or months of preparation. Others, like Isabel's snow spell, were simple enough to be explained in a few sentences. Leo saw cakes that had something to do with babies (delivering them?

caring for them? making them? Leo wasn't sure) and pies that would help with training pets. Not everything required baking, but every recipe made something sweet.

Leo flipped between the dictionary and the recipes, marveling at all the things her family's magic could do. It made her fingers itch. She couldn't wait until morning, much less until she was in high school. She needed to try these recipes now. She needed to bake.

The picture that finally caught and held her attention was a flock of pigs with wings flying off a baking tray. The recipe was for galletas voladoras. "Galleta" meant cookie, and Leo recognized the puerquitos, pig-shaped brown-sugar cookies, in the illustration. She flipped to the almost-back of the Spanish-English dictionary. "Volador" meant flying.

Flying cookies couldn't be too much harder than flying flour, Leo thought.

Under her bed, Leo found the Easy-Bake Oven she had begged for on her sixth birthday. All her sisters were allowed to use the kitchen oven by that time, and Leo had been tired of being the only one who couldn't bake things on her own. Plugging the oven's short cord into the socket next to her bedside table, Leo was pleased to see that the lightbulb inside still worked. The plastic toy oven would help Leo keep up with her older sisters again.

Leo would never get away with sneaking into the kitchen and rummaging through the pantry in the middle of the night, but her Easy-Bake Oven came with powdered cookie mixes in tiny paper packets. Isabel had said that magic was mostly about your heart, though Leo would have preferred making a batch of real puerquitos.

Leo snuck halfway down the hall to the bathroom (much safer than the kitchen for late-night excursions). As she filled a pink plastic cup with water, she jumped at every creak and splash, and when she turned around and saw a pair of glowing eyes staring from the hallway, she nearly jumped out of her skin.

It was only Señor Gato. Leo wondered briefly if he was magic too (Weren't black cats supposed to be? Would Señor Gato tell Mamá?), but he simply jumped onto the counter and rubbed his back against her elbow in lazy circles.

"You'd better not be a spy." She shook her finger at the cat, who meowed and batted at her hand. After a few scratches behind his ears, Leo returned safely to her room with the water and closed the door behind her.

Ripping the cookie mix open sent yellow dust floating across Leo's floor. She tried using Isabel's spell to clean the mess, but she was too excited to concentrate on snow. Instead, while she poured cookie powder and water into one of the plastic Easy-Bake mixing bowls, she tried to fill her mind with memories of flying dreams and trampolines and watching hummingbirds buzz around the sugar-water feeders Daddy put out in the front yard every spring.

When the dough was soft enough to shape, she popped a pinch into her mouth as a test; it tasted like super-sugary chemicals. Store-bought mixes were nowhere near as good as Mamá's recipes, but if magic came from sweetness, then Leo was sure that these cookies would hold their fair share of magic. She added two more packets of mix powder and the rest of her water until she had enough dough for a whole batch of cookies. Then she took a small ball of it and started to shape the miniature oval that would become the body of the pig.

To make the real cookies, Mamá used a rolling pin and cookie cutters. Cutting the cookies was one of the first things Mamá ever let Leo do in the bakery. Leo remembered how she had cut carelessly, making a whole tray of puerquitos that were missing limbs, ears, or tails. Mamá had baked and sold them anyway, advertised as "Leo's Lucky Pigs." Now Leo didn't have cookie cutters, but she had no trouble shaping the miniature snouts and ears, and she added tiny dough wings over the shoulders of the pigs to make them true flying cookies.

As Leo slid the first cookie into the tiny slot in the Easy-Bake Oven, she closed her eyes and thought about flight again. She was almost sure she felt a tingling in the back of her throat, a sense that she was really working magic. But it was hard to tell if she was imagining it.

She set the timer on the plastic oven and bounced up and down on her heels. The moon hid behind a cloud, shrouding everything except for the glowing white and pink plastic. The air filled with the smell of sweet warm dough and spicy magic. Leo pulled her knees up to her chest and smiled.

The cookie came out of the oven a little brown around the edges but golden and puffy in the center. Leo took the plastic spatula and pried one leg off the hot pan, careful not to push too hard and snap the limb clean off.

The freed leg wiggled. Leo yelped and dropped the spatula. The leg wiggled again, and then the other leg pulled free of the pan, and then the cookie shook itself out and stood with its thin blobby legs wobbling under it. It shook its wings, lifted its snout toward the ceiling, and leaped into the air. Leo covered her mouth so her giggle wouldn't wake her family.

"Come here, pretty," Leo whispered, but the pig ignored her and flew clumsily toward her bedside table. "Hey, don't go over there. You'll get crumbs on my books!" Leo pulled her copy of *Matilda* out from under the sugar pig. "Now stop that. Hey! That's my pillow. Don't you listen?"

The pig continued digging its snout into her pillow as though rooting for food. Maybe the pig didn't speak English? "Ven," Leo tried, and stretched out her arms, like Abuela used to when Leo was small. The pig raised its snout and turned toward her. "Ven aquí."

The little pig jumped into the air and flew onto Leo's raised palm.

"Bonita." Leo ran a finger over the pig's back while a crack appeared across the cookie's face—the pig looked exactly like it was smiling. "Okay, go on." She tossed the cookie into the air and let it explore her dollhouse. "Let's make you some brothers and sisters. Hermanos," she added, and the pig flew in spirals up toward the ceiling. Leo took this as a sign of approval.

By the time Leo's alarm clock read 12:35, six sugar cookie pigs fluttered around the room, poking their snouts into corners and showering crumbs when they bumped into one another. Leo reminded herself to find an excuse to sweep in the morning, because the last thing she needed was ants. She was holding the first pig in her hand—and looking up Spanish commands so she could train it to sit and possibly roll over—when she noticed the other five cookies crowding around the stack of books balanced on the corner of her bedside table.

"What are you doing?"

The pigs rushed the pile and, with more force than Leo would have thought their crumbly bodies could handle, shoved the books off the table and onto the ground with a loud *thump*.

"Hey!"

The pigs spiraled around the fallen books, shaking off crumbs in what looked suspiciously like silent laughter. The pig on Leo's palm jumped off to join them.

"Stop it," Leo scolded quietly, waving her hands to disperse the pigs. "Um, para. Paren, all of you! ¡Todos!"

The cookies moved out of her reach and circled one of Leo's dolls, a plastic princess whose flexible limbs hung off the edge of the shelf. "Don't you dare," Leo warned, but the pigs crashed straight into the doll, knocking her down in another noisy clatter.

"Cut it out!" Leo waved her arms more dramatically now, trying to grab the cookies as they danced out of her grasp. "Ow! ¡Paren! ¡Paren!" The cookies attacked Leo's hair and left crumbs on her nose and eyelashes as she continued swatting at them. "¡Paren! ¡Siéntense! Why won't you *listen*?"

"Leo?"

She froze at the sound of a voice outside her door. The cookies also stopped their attack, turning their snouts toward the door. Leo had just enough time to kick the spell book under the bed, but it hardly mattered, because her door had no lock and there was Marisol blinking through puffy sleepy eyes at the scene before her. At her feet sat Señor Gato, looking a little too pleased with himself.

Marisol's eyes moved across the room, landing on Leo—out of bed—the Easy-Bake Oven, and finally the flying cookies. The first pig cookie with the burned edges, snout pointed up at Marisol, darted to the wall, knocking Leo's guardian-angel plaque off its hook. Señor Gato swiped at the air, but the cookie was too quick for him. Leo winced.

Marisol sighed and rolled her eyes. "Hold on. I'll be right back."

She returned a moment later with an empty shoe box and a grim expression. Leo and Marisol herded the cookies into a corner and scooped them into the box before they could knock over anything else.

"Silencio." Marisol closed the lid on the cookies. "Tranquilo."

Either the cookies listened or the spell worked, because after a few crashes, the box went still. Leo let out a sigh of relief. Marisol turned to her and raised an eyebrow. "You want to explain how this happened, cucaracha?"

Marisol's intimidating big-sisterness didn't work like Isabel's, which made Leo feel guilty. Instead, Marisol had a way of making Leo realize exactly how silly she was being, which was an even worse kind of embarrassment. Marisol's face always seemed to ask, "Do you try hard to be this annoying, or does it come naturally?"

"Isabel told me about magic," Leo blurted. It probably wasn't right to tell on her sister, but the secret was out already. "She showed me spells."

"Uh-huh." Marisol's expression did not change. "So Isabel knows about you making flying pigs when you should be in bed asleep?"

Leo hesitated.

"That's what I thought." Marisol sat on Leo's bed, almost crushing Señor Gato, who mewed angrily and dashed into the closet. "Flying cookies," she said, tapping the box in her lap. "Always a fun one. What else have you tried?"

Leo wasn't sure if this was a trick. Was Marisol going to get Leo in more trouble if she said she had done more spells? Would she make fun if Leo said she hadn't done anything more exciting?

"Just flour snowflakes," Leo answered honestly. "Isabel taught me."

"Of course." Marisol's face turned stormy, and she stomped her feet on the floor. She must have seen Leo jump, because she laughed and shook her head. "Sorry. I'm not angry with you, cucaracha. I just think it's funny that you're the perfect little Isabel clone that everyone always wanted me to be."

Leo didn't know what to say. Nobody expected Marisol to be Isabel. Nobody expected Marisol to be anything, except maybe a little more respectful to Mamá and Daddy.

"Oh, Marisol, if you would only practice more." Marisol imitated Isabel's bossy voice. "She must be thrilled that you already want to learn, huh?"

Leo shrugged. "She told me to wait."

"And then gave you recipes to try out." Marisol rolled her eyes. "Before you even know your birth talent. Or did you get the power of influence too?"

Leo blinked wide eyes at Marisol. "I don't know. . . ."

Marisol huffed. "What? Isabel didn't tell you about birth order?"

Leo opened her mouth but then closed it and just shook her head.

"Well, let me tell you a little something, since we're throwing tradition out the window, cucaracha. For generations, Mamá's family has had daughters only. Each group of sisters gets certain magical talents based on the order in which they were born. Second-borns like Mamá and me have the power of manifestation, which means we can produce objects—small ones, for the most part—whenever we need them."

Leo gasped as Marisol opened both of her palms to reveal a purple lighter and a tube of bright-red nail polish. For years Leo had suspected her sister of shoplifting, but it had been magic all this time. She thought of Mamá's constant supply of reading glasses and mechanical pencils and couldn't help bouncing on her heels, wondering if she would get to do anything like that. "And the other sisters?"

"The third-born daughters have the power of communication. They can speak with the dead—that was Abuela, and Tía Paloma, and Alma and Belén both. Twins share a spot, I guess." Marisol flipped her suddenly empty hands over and tapped her fingers against the shoebox. "First-borns like Isabel get the freakiest power: influence."

Leo didn't think anything could be freakier than speaking to the dead, but she listened anyway.

"They make . . . suggestions. They can change a person's feelings, make you happy or sad for no reason. If Isabel ever tries to use it on you, you might not even realize it. In fact, she probably already has."

Leo shrank away. She didn't like the angry look in Marisol's eyes or the thought of someone manipulating her feelings. But she took a breath, thinking about how Isabel could always calm Alma and Belén's bickering matches and could sometimes even get Marisol to cheer up. Isabel was the family peacemaker, and that wasn't such a freaky talent.

"What about me? What talent do fourth-borns have?"

"Well . . ." Marisol made a hair tie appear on her wrist and then pulled her loose waves into a bun. "We don't really know. Each generation as far back as we can remember has had only three daughters.

Nobody had ever had twins, but Alma and Belén answered the question of what happens in that situation. But you—you're the real mystery."

"There have only ever been three daughters?" Leo knew Mamá had two sisters (though Tía Isabel had passed away when she was young). She knew Abuela had had two sisters, both much older and gone long before Leo was alive.

Marisol nodded. "For hundreds of years. If you ever get a chance, check out the genealogy in the recipe book."

Leo bit her lip. Hundreds of years, no fourth-born daughter until her. Talk about being the odd one out. "But I can do magic," she whispered firmly. Just because her birth talent was a mystery didn't mean she couldn't figure it out. Maybe it would be cooler than her sisters' powers. "I can."

Marisol made an ugly noise in her throat, and Leo felt embarrassed again.

"Sorry," Marisol said again. "For a bruja, I just don't like magic very much." Marisol turned to stare out the window so her back faced Leo. "Sure, I use it to make nail polish and little things—that's just natural, I hardly even notice that I'm doing it anymore. But I don't like using energy without knowing where it comes from. I don't like the way

Isabel always wants to use magic to fix everything. I don't like the . . . big spells. They can have terrible consequences. And if I were you, cucaracha, I wouldn't mess with any of this until I absolutely had to." Marisol turned around, sat on the edge of the bed, and patted Leo's shoulder.

Leo wasn't used to comforting gestures from Marisol. She wasn't used to Marisol talking to her in anything but sighs and eye rolls, at least for the past few years. If this conversation didn't count as magic, Leo didn't know what did.

"But if you're going to practice spells, take some advice, cucaracha." Marisol pulled her arm away and looked Leo straight in the eyes. "Follow the recipe. These little guys aren't usually so hyper, but when you use a premade mix like this, you can't really control how they'll come out. And the more complicated the spell, the more one tiny experiment can mess things up, big-time."

Leo stared. She couldn't imagine not wanting to know everything there was to know about magic. "But Isabel said that people make up new spells. She made one."

Marisol scowled. "Isabel shouldn't have told you that. She shouldn't have told you any of this. I'm supposed to be the one who rebels. Look, I don't want to be a snitch and get Mamá involved, so how about this? Don't let me catch you casting any more spells, and I'll think about keeping this between us."

Leo looked straight into Marisol's angry, scary eyes. "Okay," she lied, thinking about the spell book hidden under her feet. "No more magic."

"Good." Marisol stood up and picked up the shoe box. "And just in case you're still tempted . . ." She balanced the shoe box on top of the Easy-Bake Oven and carried them both out into the hall. "Now, go to sleep, cucaracha. No more poking around."

Leo turned out her light, crawled into bed, and pulled the covers up over her ears. She did not poke around anymore. She did not cast any more spells. But between everything Marisol and Isabel had told her, Leo had a lot to think about, and she stayed awake late into the night. She had no intention of forgetting all about magic for the next three years.

She'd just need to be quieter about it next time.

CHAPTER 10
ROLES DE CANELA

"Leo."

A soft hand shook Leo's shoulder and Mamá whispered again, "Hey, I want to talk, 'jita."

Leo bolted up in bed, a sleep-muddled confession bursting out of her mouth. "I'm sorry . . . I didn't . . . what?"

"Shh." Mamá laughed. "Calm down, sweetie. I just wanted to talk about yesterday."

Leo reached up to rub sleep from her eyes and left her hands up covering her face. Mamá knew. Maybe Marisol had gone back to her usual mean self and tattled, or maybe Señor Gato really had spied, or maybe Mamá had just used the magic of being a mom. In a very small voice, Leo said, "I'm sorry."

"It's all right, Leo. Daddy and I know you didn't mean to knock into the table."

Leo pulled her hands away from her eyes. Mamá was talking about the festival. She didn't know anything about the magic. Leo took a breath to calm her racing heart.

"I know you feel frustrated sometimes," Mamá said. "It's hard to be little and have so many older sisters. Your tía Paloma used to feel the same way. But you're worrying me, 'jita. Being rude and sulking around. So why don't you tell me what's bothering you?"

Leo hesitated. She thought that learning about the family magic would take away all her frustration, but even though she knew the secret now, her stomach still bunched up when she thought back to yesterday. "Nobody lets me do anything." A pout crept into her voice. "You never let me help."

Mamá hugged Leo around the shoulders. "We have a lot of helping hands in this family. I'm lucky to have so many wonderful daughters."

"But you didn't need so many," Leo said, thinking about generations of three daughters. But of course she couldn't tell Mamá that.

"Leonora Elena Logroño! Where did you get such a dead-wrong idea from?" Mamá jumped off the bed. "Get up. We have to do something about this."

"About what?" Leo asked. She swung her feet to the floor and checked her alarm clock. It was 5:45 a.m., a late morning for the owner of a bakery who was used to starting the day well before sunrise, but early for a sixth grader who had stayed up past midnight casting cookie spells. Leo yawned until her eyes watered and brushed wild hair out of her face.

Mamá rolled up the sleeves of her checkered pajama shirt. "Brush your teeth and meet me in the kitchen," she said. "We're making breakfast."

When Leo got to the kitchen, Mamá had shuffled clutter to leave the whole counter clear except for a silver mixing bowl and her box of index-card recipes. "What do you think, Leo?" she asked. "Crepes? Orejas? Tamales? Anything but pan de muerto— I've made more than enough of that in the past few days."

Leo perched on one of the tall kitchen stools and thought hard. She couldn't remember the last time she had gotten to decide the menu for a Sunday-morning breakfast. She couldn't remember the last time she and Mamá had been by themselves in the kitchen, without Isabel taking over most of the work or Marisol taking over most of the attention.

"Can we make cinnamon rolls?"

"Of course." Mamá reached for her box of recipes. "I have one in here with cinnamon and nutmeg, and it's wonderful. . . . Here we go." She held up a card that read *Roles de canela*.

Leo smiled. She recognized that flourished hand-writing from the recipe book. Apparently Mamá's family didn't pass down only magical recipes.

Leo hopped off her stool and stood on her tiptoes to reach the spice rack above the stove. "Cinnamon and nutmeg. What else?"

Mamá read the rest of the ingredients and Leo collected them on the counter—flour, sugar, salt, milk, butter, eggs, yeast. The ingredients stood in front of the electric mixer, ready to create a sweet breakfast. Leo's smile felt too big for her face.

"You know, Leo." Mamá measured flour in the biggest measuring cup and held out the next-biggest for Leo to measure sugar. "I'm glad that you were honest about your feelings. Sometimes Daddy and I get busy, but we love you very much."

Leo stopped scraping the top of her measuring cup flat. A familiar bad feeling bubbled up in her stomach. She hadn't been honest with Mamá at all. She had sneaked and snooped and stolen and lied. She handed Mamá the sugar to pour into the bowl. She didn't want her guilty conscience to sour the sweetness of the dough.

"Of course, I don't think that whining and stomping is a very mature way to get attention when you need it."

"I know." Leo stared at the beige linoleum floor tiles, suddenly wishing that the kitchen wasn't quite so empty.

Mamá patted Leo's hair. "I guess we'll have to find better ways to tell each other how we feel."

Leo nodded. The guilt in her stomach bubbled harder. "Mamá . . . ?"

"Yes, Leo?"

"I was wondering if you could teach me . . . I saw something that . . . Can you tell me . . ." Leo tried hard to get the words out of her mouth, but they stuck like cupcakes to an ungreased tin.

"What?" Mamá put down the milk carton and faced Leo with concerned eyes, which just made Leo feel worse.

"Can you show me . . ." Leo's courage failed. "Um, how to break an egg one-handed?"

"Of course." Mamá laughed. She grabbed one of

the eggs from the counter and whacked it expertly against the edge of the mixing bowl, dumping out the insides in one fluid shake. "But it's more about practice than teaching. Go ahead, try one. You'll have to work at that if you're going to be a baker."

Leo picked up an egg and tapped it against the bowl, so lightly at first that it didn't even crack. Mamá was right. She was going to be a baker like the rest of her family, and she was going to be a witch. A bruja, Isabel had said. She had to practice as much as possible.

Mamá watched Leo crack the rest of the eggs, and then showed her how to add flour to the batter slowly until it was real dough—springy and sticky and sweet. After they kneaded and set it aside to rise, Mamá made two mugs of hot cocoa with big puffs of whipped cream and cinnamon sprinkled on top, which they drank while preparing the second half of the recipe, the filling. Leo decided at the last minute to add a box of raisins to the cinnamon syrup, and she and Mamá stretched their dough out flat and covered it in filling before rolling the whole thing up into a swirly, gooey, spicy-smelling tube. Slicing the roll reminded Leo of how people sliced up store-bought cookie-dough tubes, except that no frozen dough could match the richness of the homemade rolls.

Leo didn't even mind that Isabel woke up in time to take over the glaze, because nobody could make sugar frosting like Isabel. By 7:45, the smell of the cooling rolls drew Daddy, Marisol, Alma, and Belén from their beds. Daddy burned his tongue being impatient and then made a show out of wincing with every bite of his next two pastries. Alma and Belén ripped one roll into small pieces and left it on a plate in the middle of the table. They offered no explanation for the extra plate, but Leo didn't have to ask what they were doing. She recognized an offering to the dead when she saw one, even without the Day of the Dead altar. Was Abuela enjoying the cinnamon rolls too? Leo smiled at the thought.

"What got you up so early, cucara—Leo?" Marisol switched nicknames when Mamá gave her a sharp look. "I thought you stayed up . . . reading . . . last night."

"I asked her to help," Mamá answered while Leo turned red and stared at the floor. "It's time she got some baking experience under her belt. Besides, she was feeling a little left out."

"Not *too* left out, I hope." Isabel drizzled sugary white frosting into a snowflake shape on her cinnamon roll and winked at Leo.

"Well, nobody is left out today." Daddy put his arm around Alma on his right and Leo on his left. "Today we celebrate a successful weekend, a bakery that actually earns money—"

"Enough money for a new house?" Mamá asked.

Daddy winked at Leo. "We also celebrate our *beautiful* house that shelters our family while we build up our savings—"

Mamá laughed and shook her head.

"—and a happy Día de los Muertos!"

Marisol rolled her eyes, Isabel laughed, and Mamá reminded everyone that they had Mass in a few hours and plenty of work waiting for them in the bakery on Monday. They all had sticky smiles on their faces. Leo licked cinnamon sugar off her fingers and smiled too, but her thoughts kept wandering to the recipe book under her bed. She didn't know what was worse, the guilty feeling of a secret or the impatience of wanting to try her next spell.

CHAPTER 11
CAROLINE'S NOTE

Before she went to bed on Sunday night, Leo climbed up on the desk part of her bookshelves and searched the highest corner, where Daddy's books from business school were lined up. She found a book on the top shelf that was thick and tall and had a dark red cover. It wasn't leather, but Leo thought it would fool a casual glance. She put the business book, the spell book, and the Spanish-English dictionary all in the inside pocket of her backpack, cramming it almost too full to carry. She would replace the empty space in the bakery office with the decoy business book as soon as possible, and keep using the recipe book to practice magic and baking. Leo packed the rest of her school things into the stuffed backpack, pleased with her plan, and went to bed.

Monday morning was hectic. Mamá left early to open the bakery, Isabel slept through her alarm, and Marisol held everyone up with an outfit emergency. Leo barely caught the school bus on time.

The bus clattered along its familiar path, and Leo reviewed her plan for the week. She would read the spell book at school, where none of her family could catch her, and translate the recipes into English in her notebook so she could try them out whenever she wanted. Leo wasn't worried about getting caught with the book at school. Ms. Wood didn't speak Spanish. She only had to worry about keeping the secret from Caroline, and that was going to be tricky.

The bus stopped at the last pickup spot. Leo looked up and spotted Brent first, then a sullen Caroline.

"Um . . . hi." Caroline slipped into the seat with Leo without glancing at Brent, who sat down at the front of the bus. She slumped into the cushion and buried her face in her hands.

"What's wrong?" Leo asked.

"I did something bad." Caroline groaned.

"What do you mean?"

"I did something weird and now Brent's not talking to me."

Leo raised her eyebrows. She couldn't imagine anything Caroline could do that would shut Brent up. "What happened?"

Caroline sniffed and dropped her hands. "It's really nothing," she whispered, spinning her green-and-white beaded bracelet around her wrist. "It's not a big deal."

Leo stayed very still and quiet, a classic Mamá technique to get people talking.

"It's just . . . ," Caroline said after a moment. "He didn't have to be so mean about it. I thought he was my friend." She buried her head in her hands and sniffed loudly.

"It's okay," Leo said. "Just tell me."

Caroline fished in the pocket of her jean overalls to pull out a crumpled piece of paper, as well as a tissue into which she blew her nose. Leo took the note (careful to avoid touching Caroline's snotty tissue), unfolded it, and read:

Dear Brent,
    This maybe seems weird, but I was just thinking that I am really glad we're friends. Today is supposed to be for

celebrating the dead, but I also wanted
to celebrate the living and tell you that
I appreciate you. Thanks for always
knowing how to cheer me up.
                              Love,
                              Caroline

Someone (not Caroline) had underlined the word
"love" three times with a smudged pencil, and the
same pencil scrawled a response underneath the
note:

ROSES R RED
VIOLETS R BLUE
GIRLS SMELL LIKE FARTS
ESPECIALLY YOU

"I was going to write one for you too," Caroline
said. "I didn't mean I *loved* him. I just meant . . ."

Leo couldn't believe it, even though the note was
right in front of her face. Brent might be a gross
boy, but he wasn't mean, not that Leo had ever seen.
"This isn't right." She looked at the note again. "He
couldn't have written this."

"I know." Caroline sniffed. "It isn't his handwriting.

I think it must be one of the boys he plays soccer with. Randall O'Connor or someone."

"Well . . . that's good, right?" Leo asked. "If he didn't write it, then there's nothing to be sad about."

Caroline shook her head, her hands rising to cover her face again. "I saw them put it in my mailbox yesterday, Leo. A bunch of the boys. Brent was there too. That means he showed it to them. He let them write it. He knew." Tears leaked down her red face, and her hunched shoulders shook. "I'm so embarrassed."

Leo crumpled the note in her fist and threw it out the window. "Brent Bayman." Each syllable of his name dripped with as much hate as she could inject into her voice. "Is a big jerkface with no personality and . . . and . . . ugly teeth!"

Caroline peeked out from between her fingertips. "His teeth are okay," she said quietly. "I mean, his braces are going to fix the gap."

He was supposed to be Caroline's friend. It made Leo's stomach churn like an electric mixer. It made her want to scream.

Caroline wiped her nose with her soggy tissue. "It was my fault," she said. "I shouldn't have written a note like that. What was I thinking?"

"Caroline," Leo said, "it is not your fault. You

did a nice thing, and you were honest about your feelings, which is a *very* adult thing to do. You are awesome."

"Thanks," Caroline said into her lap.

Leo pulled her backpack up from the floor and hugged it to her chest. She could feel the magic recipe book inside. The beginning of an idea formed in her mind. "And don't worry about Brent. . . . I'm sure he'll apologize. Maybe it was an accident, or a misunderstanding."

"Maybe." Caroline shrugged and brushed her bangs out of her red eyes. "Thanks, Leo."

Caroline wasn't her normal self during the daily math warm-up, mixing up parallelograms and quadrilaterals. She didn't raise her hand during language arts at all, even though Ms. Wood kept looking at her expectantly. Leo planned to sit with Caroline in the cafeteria and try to cheer her up, but Caroline was nowhere to be found.

Leo searched each row of gray plastic tables, double-checked the hot-lunch line, and even poked her head out into the hall without a hall pass, but in the end she was forced to sit down at her normal spot at the very end of her usual lunch table. From her seat she could smile at Tricia Morales and Mai

Nguyen, but as usual she was left out of the conversations at the center of the table.

Today, Leo didn't even try to pay attention to the laughter about whatever had happened on TV this past weekend. She was so busy checking the cafeteria doors for signs of Caroline or peeking at the spell book in her lap that she hardly even managed three bites of her sandwich, even though the long bolillo bread was fresh and fluffy. She did notice Brent sitting right in the middle of a group of boys, instead of hanging on the edge like normal.

"Looks like Brent finally stopped hanging out with Caroline."

Leo would recognize that nasal voice anywhere. *Emily Eccles.* Leo's classmate leaned crookedly over the middle of the table so everyone could see and hear her.

"Brent is cool, and Caroline . . . well . . ." Emily shrugged and flipped her curly red-blond hair. Morgan Wolfe and Taylor Rowe giggled behind their hands, nodding in agreement.

Leo clenched her fists under the table. She wished her magic powers included conjuring lightning bolts or scalding water. Across from her, Tricia shook her head, slicked-back curls bouncing, and Mai gave a sympathetic smile before the two girls turned back to their own conversation.

"Caroline is nice," María Villarreal said. The laughing stopped and the nods froze in place around her. It was the same power that had gotten her elected class president: when María talked, people listened.

"Oh, I know." Emily Eccles backtracked when she saw she was losing her audience. "She's just always been so shy. I think Brent was mostly hanging out with her to be nice, since they grew up next door to each other." A few of the other girls nodded hesitantly, but María just shrugged.

Leo took an angry bite of her ham sandwich, flipping through the pages of the spell book, hoping to find a way to turn Emily Eccles's curls into snakes and worms and creepy-crawly things. Emily Eccles didn't know anything about Brent or Caroline. She didn't know about Brent cheering up Caroline with his silly experiments, or Caroline breaking off her pan dulce for Brent, or the two of them excitedly explaining the square footage and layout of their tree-house fort.

Leo stared at the sixth-grade boys at the other table and watched Brent laugh at something Chris Robbilard had said. Emily Eccles didn't know what she was talking about. Brent might be friends with some of the worst boys in the sixth grade, but he wasn't mean like them . . . was he?

When the cafeteria started to empty about ten minutes before the bell, Leo followed the crowd to the courtyard behind the cafeteria and looked for a quiet spot to translate the spell book. Instead, she found a quiet spot that was already occupied by a quietly crying Caroline.

"Hey . . ." Leo edged her backpack onto the maroon wooden bench. "I was looking for you."

"Yeah, I didn't want to be in the cafeteria," Caroline said.

Leo nodded.

"I think everybody knows."

Leo didn't want to tell her friend that she might be right. Caroline twisted the straps of her backpack and kicked at a tuft of grass growing out from a crack in the concrete. Her eyes were still red and puffy.

Leo's fists clenched around her spell book. She didn't want to betray the family secret. Mamá and Isabel and Marisol would all be so disappointed if she told anyone, even Caroline. Not to mention what they'd think if they found out she was trying to work spells on her own.

But Brent Bayman needed a magical kick in the

rear. What was the point of having magic powers if you couldn't use them to help your friend?

"Caroline," Leo said, her voice squeaking, "what if we could get revenge?"

Caroline only sighed. "It's really nice of you to be angry, but . . . I don't want you to take it out on Brent. Please. I . . . don't want revenge, really."

"But . . ." Leo frowned. "Aren't you mad?"

Caroline ducked behind her bangs. "I don't want either of us to end up in trouble."

"But that's just it! There's no way anyone would know it was us."

"Leo." Caroline's sad voice took on a tiny bit of the confident tone she used when answering questions in class. "There's no such thing as a perfect crime. People always get caught. That's what my dad says, and he watches a lot of truTV."

"But," Leo whispered, "I bet none of those people had a top secret weapon."

"Uh-oh." Caroline's smile was tiny and watery, but it was there. "Should I be worried?"

"*You* shouldn't." Leo gave her best evil grin. The bell to signal the end of lunch rang. "Do you think it would be okay with your dad if I came over to your house after school?"

CHAPTER 12
VISITS AND SCHEMES

"Yes, Daddy can pick me up before dinner. Yes, Mr. Campbell will be home. Yes, I'll call you if I need anything." Leo hunched over and cupped a hand over her mouth. *"No,* I'm not being a bother," she whispered, sure her face turned red. "No, they don't need any scones. Well," Leo corrected herself as Caroline waved a hand, "if you want to give Daddy some scones to bring when he picks me up, that might be okay."

After answering a few more questions, Leo walked slowly with Caroline toward the curb, where their bus had just pulled up. As they reached the steps of the bus, several bodies barreled past them, a group of sixth-grade boys racing each other with no regard for safety or school rules. Randall O'Connor crashed right into Caroline's shoulder, shoving his way past her and onto the bus without an apology. Leo and Caroline glowered after him when someone else's voice said, "Oops, our bad, I—oh . . ." Leo and Caroline turned to face Brent.

He gulped, suddenly looking anywhere else. "Sorry." He stared at his shoes, then looked up at Leo, who returned his quick glance with a death glare that had him ducking his eyes right back to his sneakers. "They were just . . . sorry. I . . ." His mouth hung open until Randall O'Connor called his name, waving wildly from the front row of the bus. Brent turned and fled up the bus stairs, anything he was going to say drowned in the shrieks and laughter of the other boys.

Leo put a hand on Caroline's backpack and led her to their seats. They rode home in silence while Leo daydreamed ways to make Brent sorry he had ever messed with Caroline.

Caroline's house was only five minutes from school, and Leo was happy to get off the bus almost twenty minutes earlier than she normally did. She and Caroline worked hard to ignore Brent as he walked behind them for a block and a half, until they turned up Caroline's driveway while Brent continued to his house next door.

Caroline's house was made of red brick, newer than most of the other houses on the block, and it had two big blooming oleander bushes, one on either side of the front door. If there had been a second story, it would have been Mamá's dream house.

Leo followed Caroline through the back door and stopped.

"It's sort of messy." Caroline flipped on the kitchen light instead of opening any of the window blinds. Leo nodded and stepped around a pile of cardboard boxes sitting in the middle of the floor where the old green table normally stood. Plastic bags and Styrofoam cups from fast-food restaurants covered the counters, but Leo didn't see any pots or pans, any spatulas or knives, any spices or salt shakers.

"Dad's been doing some remodeling and changing the furniture," she said, "and we left some things in Houston."

For a second, Leo felt something prickle at the back of her throat and behind her eyes. She imagined Mamá stepping into this sad kitchen, tearing down the blinds, and rolling up her sleeves to fill it with the smell of flour and cinnamon, replacing to-go containers with pots and pans hanging from the ceiling, swapping plastic-wrapped sporks with an old cookie jar stuffed with wooden spoons, whisks, and ladles. Mamá could set everything right.

A door slammed from somewhere in the house and a voice called out, "Caro-lion, is that you?" Caroline's dad clomped into the kitchen, wearing a smile brighter than the ceiling lamps. "You're home!" He wrapped Caroline up in a bear hug and lifted her feet off the ground. "Love you, sweetie. How was your day?"

"Da-ad." Caroline swung her feet until she was set back down to stand on them. Her embarrassed grimace didn't completely hide her smile. "I brought Leo home, so you have to act normal, okay?"

Leo looked up—way up—at Mr. Campbell. "Hi, Mr. Campbell." She waved. "Is it okay that Caroline invited me over?" She smiled too, and the kitchen didn't seem like such a tragedy now that it was full of smiling faces.

"Of course! Happy to have you." Mr. Campbell held out a huge hand for Leo to shake. Caroline got her height from him, and her blond hair and big hazel eyes. "It's been too long." He smiled. "And how was your Monday, Caroline? Any news?" He smiled at Caroline, whose face fell almost immediately.

"No, Dad, nothing," she said in a voice that begged not to be asked anything else.

"Nothing?" he asked, eyebrows scrunching to match Caroline's frown.

"Nothing," she said. "I . . . I don't want to talk about it."

"Oh." Mr. Campbell hesitated, then patted Caroline's shoulder. "Well, things will look up, I'm sure. What are you two up to this afternoon?"

"We're not up to anything," Caroline answered too quickly. "Just doing stuff. For class. Homework things."

Mr. Campbell looked from his daughter to Leo and raised an eyebrow. "All right. Have fun. And please don't burn the house down with any of your . . . homework things."

Leo giggled, remembering the time they had tried to roast mini marshmallows over matches in Caroline's backyard. She followed Caroline out of the kitchen and into the hall, but not before she saw Mr. Campbell open the refrigerator to reveal an assortment of to-go containers, tapioca pudding cups, and a bag of preboiled, prepeeled eggs.

The hallway was too quiet. Would Caroline's home ever feel right again without her mom? Maybe it took more time to fill up a house with new memories. Maybe in a few years, the kitchen and hallway wouldn't feel even the tiniest bit sad anymore. Leo hoped not, anyway.

"I moved my bedroom," Caroline explained when Leo turned the wrong way down the hall. She led Leo to the right and down the hallway to the old guest room, which now had a bright-pink butterfly painted right on the door. "My dad has gotten into art," Caroline said with a shrug, and then she opened her door and waved Leo into her room.

It was bright, and messy, with pale-pink walls and a creamy yellow ceiling. The white lacy bed looked like a perfectly frosted tres leches cake. Caroline's walls held real paintings that had the same rounded shapes and bright colors as the butterfly on the door. On her bedside table stood a picture of her dad with a huge smile and huger glasses, standing next to her mom with a hospital gown and a tiny pink baby in her arms. Leo couldn't help staring at how much Mr. Campbell's face had changed in eleven years.

"So . . . do you like it?" Caroline asked.

"Yeah, of course!" Leo said. The only thing she hated more than feeling sad was having other people feel sad for her, and she didn't want Caroline to know how sad Leo felt for the small Campbell family in the picture. Leo let herself stare at the picture for three seconds. One for Mr. Campbell, whose smile had no lines of worry; two for tiny baby Caroline, who was sound asleep and smiling; and three for Mrs. Campbell. Then she turned and looked at real-life Caroline and refused to let any sadness into her voice. "It looks great."

"So, what's your plan?" Caroline asked. "You said you had a secret weapon."

"Yes, I did." Leo took a deep breath. It wasn't so bad to reveal the secret, she tried to convince herself. After all, some people in town had to know already, so they could call and order special spells. So telling Caroline was really just finding new customers, which Mamá had to approve of . . . right? Besides, Caroline could keep a secret. That's what friends did.

"Caroline," Leo said, leaning close to her friend and using her most serious and important announcement voice. "There's something you need to know about my family. We don't just bake. We also . . . do magic."

"Huh?" Caroline asked.

"Uh . . . magic," Leo repeated. "My family does magic. We're witches. Or, um, brujas."

"Oh." Caroline tilted her head. "Okay. You mean

that religious thing? My aunt lights candles for us, and she gave my mom oils and stuff to help with the chemo sickness." Caroline shrugged. "It's nice."

Leo hadn't expected a shrug.

"I'm not talking about that." She frowned. She knew about veladoras—friends and relatives from both sides of her family always had several of the tall glass candles burning somewhere in their houses. Those were good for prayers, but they weren't a secret. They also didn't short-circuit lightbulbs or make ghosts talk. "It's not like—well, we do use candles, but . . . it's baking, and it's different, and it's awesome and . . ." Leo stopped waving her hands and took a breath. "And I can show you."

Leo took a seat at the edge of the bed and pulled her backpack off her shoulders and onto her lap. She carefully unzipped the inside pocket of her backpack and pulled the spell book out. She spread it open on the bed between them, the title page releasing the familiar smell of flour and old paper. A crackly thunderstorm feeling settled into the room. The curtains stopped fluttering. Everything went quiet.

"Wow," Caroline whispered. "What is that?"

That was the reaction Leo had been looking for. "It's a spell book," she whispered back. "It's really old, and it has all the magic recipes invented by my great-great-grandma and lots of people in my family, all the way down to my sisters. Our own special magic. *Recipes of Love, Sugar—*"

"*—and Magic.*" Caroline clapped her hands. "Can I touch it?"

"Sure." Leo leaned back and let Caroline flip through the yellowed pages. "Just be very careful," she couldn't resist adding. She liked having something special that other people had to be careful with. It made her feel special too.

"This isn't exactly proof." Caroline paused to inspect a page with her eyebrows drawn together. "But it's really cool, Leo. Is it true?"

Leo searched her brain for a way to get Caroline to believe her. "Do you have any flour?"

"Um . . ." Caroline glanced toward the hallway, and Leo remembered the empty kitchen. "I don't think so."

"Sugar?" Leo asked. Caroline shook her head. "Or maybe bread?" According to Isabel, the snowflake spell was easy to modify, and Leo had already succeeded in making cookies fly without the proper recipe.

"We ran out this morning. I think there's leftover crusts in my lunch box." Caroline pulled the soft purple bag onto the bed and fished out the edges of a sandwich made on store-bought white bread.

Leo frowned. As ingredients went, dried up and factory made didn't sound promising. But crumbs could work, maybe. They sort of looked like snow.

"Okay." She crumbled the crust into smaller and smaller pieces in her palm. "This . . . should work. Um . . . prepare to be amazed." She closed her eyes, grasped at the feeling of snow and magic that had carried her flour snowflakes, and blew on her hand. The crumbs flew up into the air and then down onto Caroline's bed, exactly how crumbs would without any magic whatsoever.

"Um." Caroline frowned and brushed the crumbs into a pile. "Was that supposed to . . . ?"

Leo's face heated. "Wait, wait. One more time." She gathered up the crumbs, cheeks burning under Caroline's confused stare. *Come on.* She glared at the crusts in her hand, concentrating on the spark she had felt with Isabel, the feeling of magic lighting up her breath. This time, she imagined a winter blizzard, the biggest snowstorm anyone had ever seen. Her body tingled as she blew on her palm again.

The crumbs shot into the air. Caroline, who had been leaning closer with her eyebrows scrunched skeptically together, toppled backward as the clumps of dried bread exploded like fireworks in bright red and yellow pops of spicy-scented magic. A sticky warm hail pelted the bed, the floor, and the girls. Leo clapped her free hand over her mouth to cover her squeak.

"Oh my . . ." Caroline gulped and wiped her face.

"I'm sor—"

"Leo, this is amazing!"

"It is?" Leo closed her hanging mouth and swallowed. No need to explain what the spell *should* have done. The important thing was that Caroline had her proof. She smiled. "I told you so."

Caroline reached for the spell book, touching the pages carefully now, as though they might explode at any moment. "Well," she said after a few tense breaths, "what were you thinking, exactly?"

"I was thinking," Leo said while Caroline continued to flip through the pages, "there's a recipe to grow hair in here. . . . I bet we could try doing it backward to make all of Brent's hair fall out." That would mean more experimenting, though, and her pulse was still racing from the accidental explosion. "Or we could look for other recipes that do bad things. There must be some good curses in here—"

"Leo, no," Caroline said. "I still don't want revenge. It's not . . ." She wilted, just a little. "It's not

Brent's fault, really." Caroline shrugged. "I just wish there was a way to fix it. Are there any memory-erasing spells in this book?"

"Oh." Leo's mouth hung open in surprise. "I'm not sure." She hadn't thought of making people forget all about the note. Could she do that with magic?

"Or . . . ," Caroline said, so quietly that Leo almost missed it.

She stopped flipping pages. "Or what?"

"Um . . ." Caroline twisted her bracelet around her wrist. "I was just wondering if there was a spell in there for . . . for making somebody . . . you know. Making somebody like you more. Or like you again. Or something."

Leo hadn't thought of that either. "You want to make Brent *like* you? Are you sure you wouldn't rather make his hair fall out?"

Caroline turned as pink as her door. "I meant what I said in that note. He's one of my best friends, and I . . . I just want us to be okay again."

"You didn't make it not okay. Brent did."

"But we've known each other forever, and he's so nice most of the time. And I like talking to him, and he reads almost as much as I do, and he let me into his tree house, even though it's supposed to be boys only."

Leo squinted at Caroline. She thought she recognized that moony look in her friend's eyes. It was the same look Marisol had when she talked about Jonathan García, the boy with the leather jacket who worked the cash register at his parents' music store.

Maybe Caroline hadn't written "love" for no reason after all?

Leo still didn't understand why Caroline wanted anything to do with Brent after that nasty note. But then she thought about Brent and Caroline laughing at the festival, about how Caroline said he came over every day to cheer her up. Maybe he wasn't so bad, even if he did have horrible taste in friends. Maybe he only needed a little bit of magical help to stand up to those boys and act nicer to Caroline. If Leo could do that, she could make both of them happy, probably.

"We will definitely find something," Leo promised. "We can pick a recipe right now. I'll just have to look up the words. . . ." She pulled the Spanish-English dictionary out of the inside pocket and then let the backpack flop onto the floor, lighter now with just Leo's school notebooks and Daddy's decoy book.

Caroline waved her hand when Leo tried to offer the dictionary. "I'm pretty good at Spanish now.

I've been studying all summer, especially since . . . You know, I want to stay connected to her. Now my grandma only speaks to me in Spanish when I call her in Costa Rica."

"Really?" Leo sighed in relief. "It's been taking me forever to look things up."

Caroline beamed and turned to the recipe book. "Let's see . . . we have pan de muerto . . . truth tarts . . . and look at this one here. I'm hungry enough to eat a tamale that will turn me into an elephant!" She pointed at the recipe for Tamales de transformaciones.

"I think I remember one," Leo said, pulling the book back toward herself. "Something about friendship . . ."

She found the page, and she and Caroline stared at the two women hugging over their tea.

"They . . . look sort of old," Caroline said. "I'm not sure I could even get Brent to drink tea."

Leo nodded. The page reminded her of Mamá's arguments with Tía Paloma, the kind that meant screaming and always needed to be smoothed over. It didn't feel right for Caroline at all.

"Maybe we can keep looking?" Caroline suggested, flipping more pages.

Leo giggled. "Hey, what about this?" She pointed

to a page with hearts drawn on it before Caroline could flip too quickly past it.

MORDIDAS DE AMOR
UNA MORDIDA DE ESTAS GALLETAS DELICIOSAS LLENARÁ AL CORAZÓN DEL SUJETO CON CARIÑO

"Love bites," Caroline read. "'Just one bite of these delicious cookies will fill the subject's heart with affection.'" She scrunched her nose and stuck out her tongue at Leo.

Leo thought she should have understood most of that on her own, but it was convenient to have Caroline translate. "Affection sounds good," she said, a sneaky thought working its way into her mind. Caroline really seemed to like Brent a lot. Maybe a love spell was exactly what they needed.

"*Love* cookies?" Caroline asked, her face doubtful. "That word is what got me into this mess in the first place."

"You're the one who said you wanted Brent to like you." Leo shrugged. "It will probably work for any kind of love."

Caroline bit her lip. "My grandma does call me 'cariña' . . . so it can't be too romantic, right?"

"Exactly," Leo said. "This one definitely feels

right." And if, as she suspected, Caroline had a little bit of a crush on Brent, maybe these cookies would help. "So how do we make them?"

"It looks complicated. . . ." Caroline dragged her index finger down the page. "And we need lots of things from Brent, like an eyelash and . . . his signature. That probably means in cursive, right? And we need my signature too, but that's easy. . . ."

"I'm sure we can get everything we need."

"Okay." Caroline looked up from the recipe and smiled. "If you say so. You're the expert."

"Right. Exactly." It wasn't really a lie. She had done spells before. Just maybe not ones that were this complicated. "Piece of cake."

"You mean cookies!" Caroline laughed. "But where are we going to make them? And where will we get all the normal ingredients—flour and sugar and everything? I don't think we have any of that here. My dad hasn't really felt like going to the store."

Leo felt a smile spreading across her face. "Don't worry about that," she told Caroline. "Just try to get all the things from Brent that we need, and ask your dad if you can come home with me tomorrow. Everything else will be all taken care of. . . ." Pride sent delicious goose bumps up Leo's arms and puffed her chest. "Just one thing," she added, deflating. "Um, don't tell anyone about this? Even my sisters. We have to keep it secret."

"Of course." Caroline bit her lip. "Although, if your family doesn't want you doing it . . ."

"No, no." Leo waved her arms and shook her head. "Everything is fine. Marisol thinks doing laundry is too dangerous for me. You're lucky you don't have to deal with older sisters."

"But," Caroline reminded Leo, "you have baking magic."

"That's true, and I forgot to tell you the best part! It's not just baking—I get a special mystery power when I turn fifteen, too."

She filled Caroline in on the birth-order powers, and the two of them speculated on what power Leo might have and what the best power would be (a tie between flying, telekinesis, and being able to do homework at lightning speed). They flipped through the spell book, getting almost as excited about the sweets as the spells. Caroline's new bed was soft and the sun shone warm through her window onto Leo's shoulders. She liked having her best friend back. She wanted Caroline to be happy.

Which meant that she *had* to pull off this spell.

CHAPTER 13
GINGERSNAPS

Daddy came to pick Leo up right before dinner, carrying a big basket of lemon scones. While he talked with Caroline's dad, Caroline and Leo made sure their plan for the next day was settled. Leo would be in charge of baking supplies, location, recipes, and of course the magic. Caroline would be in charge of collecting Brent's signature, his eyelash, and an article of his clothing. The plan was for Caroline to ask to borrow his sweatshirt in the morning—neither of the girls wanted to bake cookies using stolen gym socks.

Leo couldn't help smiling as she made her way to

Daddy's car. With such a foolproof plan, she couldn't wait to practice using magic again. She thought that, once Brent stopped being such a big butt and they got to high school, he and Caroline would probably fall in love for real. They would make a nice couple. They wouldn't fight like Marisol and the boys she went out with. They would be happy and read books together in tree houses. Leo wondered if they would let her bake the cake for their wedding. She would make it a very special good-luck cake, because she would be the world's most powerful bruja by then, and she would be running the bakery—with Isabel as her assistant, of course.

"Did you have fun?" Daddy asked when Leo climbed into the truck. He started the engine on the first try and pulled out of the driveway.

"It was great! I missed her." Leo flung an arm out the open window. Her entire body still bubbled with excitement.

The pickup truck made a creaking noise as they went over a speed bump on the way out of Caroline's neighborhood.

"I'm glad," Daddy said. He reached one-handed to ruffle Leo's hair. "All my girls turned out so well, I must have the best luck in the world."

Leo smiled and wondered if Daddy knew about

the good-luck bread Mamá could make. She wondered if he had ever read the family recipe book, and what he thought about marrying into a family of bakery brujas. She wondered if he really thought she had turned out well, and if he would still think so if he knew what she and Caroline were up to. . . . Leo's stomach dropped a bit as she thought about what her mom or sisters would say if they found out. But her nervousness was soon overtaken by excitement as she thought more about her and Caroline's happy future.

"¡'Jita!" Mamá wrapped Leo up in a hug as soon as she walked in the door. "Did you have a good time? Are you hungry? How's Caroline's father doing? Tell me about it."

"They're okay," Leo said. "They're redecorating. We just talked and had fun."

"Well, good." Mamá smiled at Leo. "I thought I'd let Daddy do quesadillas tonight, but if you want to help me with some dessert, we could try another recipe after dinner."

"You heard right. Famous Logroño quesadillas coming up! Please, form an orderly line, and no pushing." Daddy walked into the kitchen with his hands up to keep away imaginary fans. Marisol followed him, sighing and shaking her head.

"Actually," Leo told Mamá, "Caroline wanted to come over tomorrow and learn to make gingersnaps. They're her favorite. I want to teach her, but . . . I don't really know how to make them."

Mamá clapped her hands together. "Ooh, I love gingersnaps! And it's just in time for fall too. What a good idea, Leo."

"Gingersnaps?" Alma poked her head out of the hall, chunks of her hair wrapped in tinfoil. "Who's making gingersnaps?"

"I was going to show Leo how, so she can teach Caroline," Mamá said. "You're welcome to help after dinner if you want."

Belén poked her head out of the hallway behind Alma, her hair similarly foil wrapped. "What's for dinner?"

After Daddy's famous quesadillas had been distributed, slathered in crema and pico de gallo, and devoured, Alma and Belén disappeared to their room and returned minus the tinfoil, but with several new streaks of blue and pink in their hair.

"I wish you'd give us some warning before you did that." Mamá shook her head but laughed.

"I like it." Marisol glared around the table defiantly.

"That's what worries us," Daddy teased, and then, before Marisol could get angry, he stood up and carried his dirty dishes to the sink. "Come on, everybody, pass your plates. Who's going to help me wash?"

Alma, Belén, and Leo used gingersnaps as an excuse, so while Daddy, Isabel, and Marisol cleaned the kitchen, Mamá brought her recipe box into the living room and pulled out all the gingersnap recipes she had.

"This is the one we'll use for the bakery in a few weeks." Mamá pulled out a bright white index card with a printed recipe neatly pasted onto it. "It's pretty basic, but the cookies turn out perfectly and they hold shapes well."

"What about this one?" Leo held up a card that had bent corners and yellowed edges and was written in cramped cursive Spanish. She had studied both the handwriting and the directions for the magic cookies at Caroline's house, and this recipe was almost the same, though noticeably missing eyelashes from the list of ingredients.

A funny smile crept onto Mamá's face. "Oh, that old recipe." She laughed. "Sure, we can try that one. It makes the cutest little cookies."

Leo shrugged, hoping that Mamá didn't think

too hard about why Leo might have chosen that particular recipe. Alma and Belén looked at each other, raising their eyebrows. Alma asked, "What's so funny?"

"Oh." Mamá waved a hand at the twins. "When I was in high school, I—I made these cookies for a boy I liked." Mamá actually giggled and even looked like she might be blushing. "It didn't turn out exactly how I wanted it to, but . . . well, I had to try. He was such a sweet young man, and *so* handsome. Or . . . what do you kids say? Hot. He was very *hot.*"

"Mamá!" Belén covered her mouth with her hands. Alma laughed until her face turned almost as pink as her hair. Leo tried not to look too suspicious, but she couldn't help laughing too. Mamá had used the love bites recipe on that boy, Leo was sure of it. Learning to make the perfect mordidas de amor was going to be even easier than she thought.

"So," Alma asked, "what happened?"

Mamá shook her head. "Even the best cookies can't create potential where there is none. But we became better friends after that." She smiled; then her face went serious. "I hope I never hear of any of you acting so silly." She pointed at Alma and Belén, and then at Leo. "People should like you for who you are, not for . . . any other reason. Even how well you bake."

"Uh-oh." Daddy came out of the kitchen and stood behind the couch with his hands on Mamá's shoulders. "I guess now would be a bad time to mention that I married you for your tres leches?"

Mamá swatted Daddy's hands and gathered the recipes back into the box. Leo followed Mamá into the sparkly clean kitchen, gathered all the ingredients they needed, and started filling the mixing bowl. Leo made sure to pay special attention to all the advice Mamá gave as they went along, like not stirring for too long or else the cookies would come out hard. To Leo's surprise, Alma and Belén added a few tips of their own.

"Don't forget to mince it extra fine, Elenita—uh, I mean Mamá," Belén said when Mamá reached for the ginger root.

"Oh, hush." Mama didn't look at Belén but glanced suspiciously around the kitchen like she was looking for someone. "I haven't messed up the mincing since I was twelve years old." She rolled her eyes, almost like Marisol.

Leo guessed that the tips must be coming not from the twins but from Abuela, and she secretly glanced around the kitchen looking for signs of ghostly activity. She didn't see anything, though.

When the cookies were safely in the oven, Mamá

went to the bathroom. The second she left, Alma and Belén started tugging their ears and tapping their noses at each other in their secret twin code. Leo climbed onto the stool in front of the counter, ready to leave them to their own little world, but to her surprise, Alma suddenly huffed and turned to her. "Leo, we want to talk to you. Abuela says you found out."

Leo's mouth dropped open. She thought about pretending not to know what Alma was talking about, but her curiosity got the better of her.

"How did she know that?"

"Oh, you know." Belén smiled sweetly. "Ghosts like to check in every now and then. Plus Señor Gato is a terrible gossip."

Leo had known that cat was up to no good. She was going to give him a bath the next time she saw him. "You can talk to cats?"

"Not directly, but some cats can talk to ghosts, if they feel like it," Alma said. "The stronger ghosts, mostly, like Abuela."

"Wait a minute." Leo still wasn't entirely sure how the twins' powers worked. "I thought you had to use special bread to contact ghosts?"

"That's only for the festival. We can see and talk to any of the ghosts who are hanging around, no problem. It's calling them, or channeling them so other people can hear, that takes extra effort."

As if Alma and Belén needed another reason to be lost in their own world. "And Abuela hangs around?"

Alma nodded. "She still has so much love tying her to the world of the living. The older ghosts get a little more . . . scattered, and then sometimes they stop showing up altogether—"

"But," Belén interrupted her sister, "we didn't bring this up to teach you about the finer points of ghost manifestation. We just wanted to know if finding out about magic had anything to do with your sudden interest in Mamá's old recipes."

"And more important"—Alma glared slightly at Belén—"we wanted to warn you to keep an eye out for ghosts, since no one knows what your birth power is going to be. We started noticing eyes in the corner and hearing whispers about a year ago, but it can begin earlier, and we could help you out."

Leo wanted to ask more, but Belén had already picked up speaking where Alma had left off. "Plus, we figured that you picked gingersnaps for a reason. We want to hear how the love spell goes, because it might be just the thing to get Marcus and Marcellus to notice us."

Marcus and Marcellus were the other set of identical twins at Rose Hill High School. Leo hadn't known that Alma and Belén had crushes on the sophomore brothers, but she thought it would be pretty funny if the twins paired off with each other. She also felt a swell of pride that Alma and Belén weren't trying to warn her away from doing magic. They even wanted to hear her advice once she had finished the spell.

"But mostly . . ." Alma stuck her tongue out at Belén. "We just wanted to say that we're excited. We didn't like leaving you out."

"The fifteen-years thing is silly, anyway, since we won't be fifteen for another three months," Belén added.

"And everyone keeps saying that practicing without supervision is *dangerous*," Alma said, flipping her pink-and-blue bangs with a toss of her head.

"But Tía Paloma is too strict. We barely get to do any cool spells, and nothing has even blown up or anything. I would personally like a little more danger and a little less memorizing incantations," Belén complained.

"Also," Alma added, "Abuela says you're a natural, Leo."

"So yay," Belén said.

"Now everyone knows," said Alma.

"Which is better," said Belén.

The twins looked at each other and nodded. Leo waited a minute to make sure they were really finished—sometimes when Alma and Belén both talked, they could go on for hours without letting anyone else get a word in. Right now Leo didn't find her sisters' chatter annoying, though. Relief and excitement coursed through her. Alma and Belén didn't think she was too little.

"Not everyone," she reminded them. "Mamá doesn't know."

"Doesn't know what?" Mamá appeared in the doorway, and Leo almost fell off her stool. "Don't tell me my sweet little girls are up to something."

"No, Mamá," Alma said smoothly. "We were just saying that you don't know much about hair dye. We learned about it online."

"Oh, you two." Mamá sighed. "Leo, while I appreciate your beautiful sisters' unique sense of style, I think you're a little young to dye your hair any cartoon colors, okay, 'jita?"

"Okay, Mamá." Leo laughed at the thought of her frizzy hair popping out of her head in a cotton-candy-colored swirl, but her stomach did a tiny guilty somersault. She wasn't going to dye her hair, but she was doing lots of other things Mamá thought she was too young for. Luckily, before Leo could feel too bad, the green plastic egg timer rang out and everyone got distracted taking the cookies out of the oven.

"These look delicious." Mamá smiled. "I'm so glad you picked this recipe, Leo. I missed my abuelita's cookies more than I realized."

Behind Mamá's back, Belén winked. Leo pushed down the last of her guilt and smiled. She didn't feel great keeping secrets from Mamá, but she felt a lot better than when her sisters were keeping secrets from her.

CHAPTER 14
LOVE BITE

Leo's whole body bubbled like a boiling pot when she and Caroline fell into their seats after school. Only one long bus ride stood between her and her first big spell.

"Did you get everything?" Leo asked, even though Caroline had flashed thumbs-up signs from her desk all afternoon. A thumbs-up wasn't good enough—Leo wanted definite proof that everything was going according to plan.

"I got everything. . . ." Caroline stared at the ground, twisting her bracelet and biting her lip. She didn't seem nearly as excited as Leo felt. "I couldn't get him to sign his name in cursive, because he always forgets how to make r's, but I got it in print."

The bus finally reached Leo's stop, and Leo and Caroline walked to the Logroño house. Caroline scratched Señor Gato's chin when he hopped up on the couch to greet her. "It feels like forever since I've been over, but everything's the same."

"Hello, girls." Daddy hurried out of the living room with a handful of papers in one hand and a pen tucked behind his ear. His dark hair stuck straight up, and he ran his free hand through it to make it puff even worse. "I'm having a little bit of a problem with some—well, never mind. Isabel's at the bakery with Mamá and Alma and Belén. Marisol is out with someone, doing something, until sometime tonight." He sighed. "Very nice to have you over, Caroline." He tried to shake her hand while balancing a full stack of papers.

"Daddy." Leo covered her face with her hands. "You're being weird."

"Et tu, Leo? Is my last baby turning into a surly teenager? Well, it had to happen sooner or later, I suppose. Have a good time, you two." He sighed one more time and then returned to the office.

Leo led Caroline through the dining room, a little relieved that the rest of her family wasn't home acting nosy and silly. Besides, they needed the kitchen to themselves if they didn't want to get caught.

"Wow." Caroline beamed. "I forgot how awesome your kitchen is." Leo watched her friend's eyes scan all the mixers and blenders and eggbeaters lined up along the counter, the cookie sheets and cake tins that didn't fit in cupboards stacked on top of the refrigerator.

"It is awesome," Leo agreed. "Now let's get baking."

MORDIDAS DE AMOR
UNA MORDIDA DE ESTAS GALLETAS DELICIOSAS LLENARÁ AL CORAZÓN DEL SUJETO CON CARIÑO

INGREDIENTES

2 tazas harina

1 taza de azúcar blanca

¼ taza de melaza

¾ taza de manteca

1 cucharada de jengibre molido

1 cucharadita de canela

1 huevo

2 cucharaditas de bicarbonato

½ cucharadita de sal

¼ taza de agua

1 prenda u objeto querido del sujeto

1 pestaña del sujeto

la firma del sujeto

1 pestaña de la persona que el sujeto debe amar

la firma de la personal que el sujeto debe amar

Leo scanned the recipe one last time before running to set the oven to preheat, and then she put water on the stove top to boil Brent's sweatshirt. This was the trickiest part of the recipe—not because it was hard to do, but because it was the most likely to get them caught. Daddy might not notice a scrap of autographed paper being slipped into a bowl of batter, but he would definitely notice sweatshirt soup! They had to stay on alert, and they had to act fast.

"Okay, so now I need an eyelash from you, and your autograph too," Leo said, holding out her hand.

"Leo . . . ," Caroline said, "what if this isn't a good idea?"

"What do you mean?" Leo froze. "You're here. We already started."

Caroline was staring at the book, her fingers tracing the hearts at the top of the page. "I don't want to force him to like me." She twisted her bracelet at top speed. "This was a bad idea. We should call it off."

"But . . ." Leo felt disappointment well in her stomach at the thought of abandoning her first real spell. She couldn't quit now. Caroline was probably just nervous, like Leo got before school pageants. She just needed some reassurance. "We're not going to force him," she continued. "We're just giving your friendship a little tiny jump start. Adding some affection to sweeten his personality."

"That's not how the spell works." Caroline pointed to the book. "You put in who you want them to love, and then they love that person. That's not a jump start, that's a hijack."

"Well . . . what if . . ." An idea was forming at the back of Leo's brain. "What if the spell didn't work like that?"

"What do you mean?"

Leo waited while the idea bubbled into shape. "What if we took you out of the spell?" The idea grew, and Leo's excitement grew with it. "We don't want to force him to like you, but we could make these cookies just encourage him to feel more affection in general. It'll work out the same, because you're already such good friends. I'm sure that just a little bit of love is all he needs to apologize, and then you can be friends again."

Caroline chewed her bottom lip.

"No signature from you, and no eyelash. We'll just leave that part blank. Extra cariño for whoever he already cares about, which is you."

"Is that okay? You think it will work?"

If Leo had been perfectly honest, she would have admitted that she wasn't really sure. If she had been perfectly honest, she would have mentioned Marisol's warning about experimenting with recipes, and how dangerous spells could be. But even though Leo did remember Marisol's warning, it was Isabel's encouragement and Alma and Belén's eagerness that came to her mind. If Isabel could experiment and create her own spells, then Leo could, too. Like Isabel said, it was the feeling that mattered most.

"Yes!"

Once the Brent water was ready (and the sweatshirt hung over a chair to dry), Leo started the real baking. She showed Caroline how to find what they needed in the pantry, and how to scrape the excess off the top of the measuring cups without packing down the flour too much. Caroline had a helpful knack for remembering the details of the recipe without needing to look at it over and over, so Leo could keep the spell book hidden under a large overturned frying pan while they worked. Leo and Caroline laughed when they had to add three drops of the boiled Brent-flavored water into the mixing bowl, but they couldn't resist tasting the spicy dough once it sat round and sticky and finished in the bowl.

"Okay," Leo said, "I have to do more magic now. Will you check the doors?"

When Caroline signaled that the coast was clear, Leo took a deep breath and closed her eyes. Holding Brent's stolen eyelash in one hand and his written name in the other, Leo plunged both hands into the dough.

"Brent Bayman," she whispered, and she thought about Brent with his mouth full of sweet bread, his smile when he told Caroline that he would talk to her later. She remembered the time in second grade when Brent and his mom had come into the bakery to buy a birthday flan, and his little sister had thrown a fit about wanting a real cake, and Brent had distracted her with silly faces while his mom explained to Mamá about the little girl's celiac disease. Leo didn't know Brent well, but she liked what she knew. Up until recently, at least. It wasn't hard to find enough sweet thoughts to fill the cookies up. Leo's hands tingled inside the dough, like they had fallen asleep.

"Did it work?" Caroline asked when Leo pulled

her hands free. "I didn't see anything."

"It . . ." Leo hesitated. She had only done magic a few times, and she wasn't sure if it was supposed to look like anything special. But she had felt it. "It worked," she said finally, more because she didn't want Caroline to doubt her than because she was doubt-free herself. "And this is the part where we would add your name and your eyelash, but we aren't doing that. So now we just need to shape them and bake them."

They had fun rolling bite-sized balls of dough and lining them up on the baking pan. Leo even made a few heart-shaped cookies, just to see if they would hold their shape while they baked. She thought about making a pig-shaped cookie but decided it was best not to risk it.

They'd halved the recipe but still had enough dough to fill a whole tray—twelve cookies in all. It was a lot to give to one person, but Leo didn't want to eat any of the cookies herself without knowing what effect the Brent-specific magic could have on someone who wasn't Brent. While the cookies baked, Leo and Caroline raced through their math homework, and then Caroline helped Leo with their social studies worksheet. Halfway through it, the timer rang. The smell of baking cookies already infused the kitchen, but opening the oven door let an even stronger cloud of warm spicy freshness into the air. Leo was sure she smelled magic too. She hopped up and down until she had to stop to carefully remove the hot tray from the oven with a potholder. The cookies were going to work—she could feel it.

"Looks like I came just in time." Daddy walked into the kitchen as Leo used a spatula to transfer the cookies two at a time onto the shiny cooling rack. "You girls didn't make too much of a mess, did you?" He reached for one of the still-hot cookies from behind Leo's back.

"Don't eat that!"

Daddy dropped the cookie, startled. Leo immediately wished she hadn't screamed, but she was afraid that the magic cookies might cast their spell on Daddy.

"Sorry," Leo said quickly. "We just—we need enough to give to all the people. In the club."

"The club?" Daddy raised an eyebrow. "What club is that?"

Leo opened her mouth, exactly like a goldfish and nothing like a criminal mastermind, but luckily Caroline spoke up.

"It's just a club for snacking." She bit her lip and tugged on a braid. "At lunch, we take turns bringing fun snacks. We had it at my school in Houston—I thought maybe I could start it here. That's why I asked Leo to make these cookies."

Leo quickly put on a smile and nodded like she had known about the snack club all along. Daddy smiled and reached around Leo's shoulder for a hug she knew she didn't deserve.

"I think that's a great idea, Caroline. I hope you girls are making sure to include everyone. You could have made a bigger batch if you were worried about having enough."

"Oh, we are including people." Caroline nodded. "Everyone who wanted, at least. But hopefully after this week, even more people will join."

Leo hid her laughter by moving the rest of the cookies to the rack. Caroline might be the greatest actress ever.

"If they get a whiff of these cookies, I can't imagine anyone turning you down," Daddy said. "Well, I guess I'll have to sacrifice my own rumbling stomach for the good of the snack club." He stared longingly at the cookies but walked toward the door.

"Daddy." Leo stopped him before he left.

"Mm-hm?"

"They're the same recipe we made yesterday. The leftovers are in the cookie jar. You can have as many of those ones as you want."

"Now that's what I like to hear." Daddy pulled the head off the teddy bear cookie jar that sat on the windowsill year-round in spite of its Christmas sweater. He fished out three of yesterday's cookies, two of which he offered to Leo and Caroline. "Cheers, girls."

They each took a bite.

"Like I said." Daddy gave a happy sigh. "Your club will explode with members after they taste these cookies. You girls are destined for success."

Even though the club wasn't a real club, even though it was just a sneaky lie between sneaky friends, Leo hoped he was right.

CHAPTER 15
FRIENDS AND FAMILY

After some debate, Leo and Caroline decided to leave three cookies in Brent's locker. They didn't want to risk him sharing with anyone, but they were afraid that one tiny cookie wouldn't be enough.

Leo wrapped up the cookies using the clear plastic bags and golden twist ties that Mamá kept at home, even though they were really for bakery products. Caroline wrote a mysterious note ("Hope you have a sweet day!") in curly cursive that didn't look anything like her normal handwriting. The rest of the cookies Leo hid in a big Ziploc bag under her bed until she could ask Alma and Belén's advice on what to do with them. She didn't want to toss them—Mamá hated wasted food—but she wasn't sure they were safe to leave lying around. If Alma and Belén didn't know, maybe Abuela would.

At lunch on Wednesday, Caroline asked for permission to go to the library to check out a book for a made-up project. Leo ripped crumbs off the fresh fluffy bread of her sandwich, barely able to sit still knowing that Caroline was sneaking down the sixth-grade hall to tape the cookies to Brent's locker door. Leo tapped her foot under the long gray lunch table and shifted on the attached plastic stool. What would happen if Caroline got caught? What was taking so long?

"Is everything okay?"

Leo jumped. Mai Nguyen frowned at her, head tilted like Señor Gato when he caught Leo staring at him.

"Oh, yeah, everything's fine," Leo said after a pause.

"Where's Caroline?" Tricia tilted her head at the empty seat beside Leo.

"She's . . ." Leo had planned to say "at the library," but she didn't have to, because at that moment, Caroline pulled open the cafeteria door and flashed Leo a thumbs-up from behind Tricia's and Mai's backs. "She's right there."

The girls turned, and Leo sighed and dropped her handful of crumbs so that she could take her first real bite out of her ham sandwich. Caroline grinned as she sat down and pulled her lunch bag out of her backpack. "Mission accomplished," she whispered to Leo.

"Oh, good." Tricia flashed a smile at Caroline. "We were afraid you were going to miss lunch because of those gross boys again."

Mai nodded. "We wanted to tell you that we think what they did was horrible. Boys are jerks."

"Oh." Caroline blushed deep red. "Thanks." She shifted on her cafeteria stool.

"We also wanted to say welcome back." Mai smiled. "How are you doing?"

"I'm okay. I'm good. I've been hanging out with Leo. She's teaching me how to bake."

"Wow!" Tricia took a big bite out of her tuna sandwich and scattered crumbs as she talked. "That is so cool. Leo's family makes the best bread in the whole state, probably. You must be an expert baker, right, Leo?"

Leo ducked her head and smiled into her lunch box. She didn't know Tricia was so into the bakery. Leo liked Mai and Tricia, but she never knew what to say to them. The two girls had been best friends with each other all through elementary school, and they fit together like matching salt and pepper shakers.

"I always get my birthday cake from your bakery," Mai added. "I saw you working at the Day of the Dead festival, but you were talking to your sister and you didn't see me." Mai stopped and looked embarrassed.

"I'm sorry," Leo said. "I would have said hi if I'd seen you. I guess I was just a little . . ."

"Distracted," Mai said. "We know." She and Tricia shared a smile.

"You're always in your own world," Tricia said with a nod.

"Yeah, but Leo's world is way cooler," Caroline said.

"I want to hang out there," Tricia said.

"You should let us in sometime." Mai smiled at Leo.

Leo dropped her head. She had always thought that she had problems making friends because it was such a difficult thing to do; she had never considered that there might be friends to be had if she had just looked a little harder.

"I want to learn some baking too," Tricia said. "It sounds awesome."

"It is awesome." Caroline raised her head a little and smiled. "Actually . . . we were talking about doing a thing where . . ." Her eyes flickered to Leo. "Where we all take turns making cookies and bringing them for everyone to eat. Like a club. A snack club. If you two would be . . . I don't know, interested in that."

Tricia and Mai were in love with the idea of a snack club, and their excited questions attracted the attention of other sixth graders sitting near them. Soon Leo had promised to bring cookies for everyone at the table one week from Friday, and Mai had offered to bring in muffins for the Friday after that.

Leo had never been the center of so much attention. Her cheeks flushed as she made up the answers to questions about the club—how many servings did you have to bring? Did everything have to be homemade? Would eighth graders be allowed in, or boys? Leo felt a little nervous about all the talking and laughing until she caught Caroline's eye and saw her friend looking a little overwhelmed too. Leo laughed, and Caroline laughed, and soon the whole table was laughing.

Leo half wondered if she had cast some sort of accidental bread-crumb spell for popularity, but she knew that there was a different kind of magic happening at the table. All year Leo had felt shy and left out, but with Caroline back at her side, talking felt simple. Maybe having one friend made it easier to make more.

"I *have* to tell you what happened," Caroline said when she and Leo had a minute alone in the courtyard. "I was walking past Brent's locker, ready to leave the cookies, when I saw Brent walking straight toward me! I got so scared, I hid behind the water fountain. Brent should have seen me, but he didn't, and he still didn't see me when I peeked over the top of the water fountain a minute later. He grabbed a few things out of his locker, but then he just stopped moving and stared at the locker for a long time, and then he closed the door and walked away *without even locking it*. He looked like a zombie or something, and his face was all pale."

"Weird," Leo said. "Do you know why?"

"No." Caroline shrugged and frowned. "But he left the locker open, so I put the cookies right inside and locked them up. I was so lucky."

Leo nodded as the bell rang and crowds in the courtyard surged into the hallway. The plan had worked even more perfectly than they had imagined. She did feel lucky.

Of course, as soon as Leo thought this, the plan's luck ran out. Brent's seat, when she returned to Ms. Wood's classroom to start science, was mysteriously empty, and some of the boys around Leo whispered that Brent had thrown up in the locker room after gym and had gone home.

Leo's throat turned dry as she tried to hear more of the whispers. Had Brent found the cookies before he left? With no way to know, Leo chewed on her lip and tapped her fingers on her desk. From Caroline's nervous face in the front of the room, Leo guessed that her friend had heard the same rumor and was wondering the same thing.

The two girls sat quietly through the bus ride that afternoon, Leo tapping her fingers and Caroline tugging her braid and twisting her bracelet. Leo opened her mouth at least five times to say something, but every time, she stayed silent, worried that someone would overhear her if she mentioned Brent, magic, or cookies.

At home, Leo stomped around restlessly until she scared Señor Gato out of the living room. She moved to the kitchen and paced, counting and recounting the steps between the table and the refrigerator.

"Everything okay, Leo?" Daddy interrupted her path to get orange juice out of the fridge. "How did your cookies go over?"

Leo startled before she remembered the snack club lie. At least she had real news to share now instead of having to make up more lies. "It was great. I think a lot of people are interested."

As soon as Daddy left the kitchen, Leo resumed her pacing.

"Hey, little Leo." Isabel snuck two gingersnaps out of the cookie jar and ate them standing over the counter. "What are you up to?"

Leo stopped pacing but continued tapping her fingers against her shorts and tapping her toes on the floor. "Oh, nothing. I'm just . . ." Isabel chomped into her second cookie and smiled, ready to listen. Leo could tell Isabel what was going on. Alma and Belén already knew. Isabel wouldn't get mad, probably.

Unless she did get mad. Unless she thought Leo shouldn't be telling family secrets.

"Isabel," she said, "have you ever . . ." She couldn't risk telling Isabel everything, but she wanted her sister's reassurance. "What do you do when you're worried?"

Isabel sat across the table from Leo, bringing the cookie jar and setting it between them. "That depends," she said. "What are you worried about?"

"Nothing. Nothing really. It doesn't even matter."

"Well." Isabel leaned forward on her elbows. "If I don't know what I'm worried about, sometimes it helps to talk about it."

Leo shook her head. Leo wanted to see the results of her spell, and not even Isabel's encouragement could scratch her impatient itch. Either the spell would work or it wouldn't, and until she knew, Leo couldn't stop being excited and nervous and guilty and proud.

"Never mind. There's nothing I can do about it anyway."

"In that case . . ." Isabel sat up straight, pulled her hair away from her face, and closed her eyes. "You should probably relax."

Leo's heart stopped pounding, and the butterflies in her stomach folded their wings. A dizzy fizzing in her brain almost distracted her from the spicy scent that wasn't coming from the gingersnaps.

"That's magic." She grabbed the table to steady herself. "You're using magic on me." This was Isabel's power of influence, changing Leo's feelings.

"Yes, sorry. I thought it might help. Do you mind?"

Leo shrugged as the fuzziness faded. She couldn't be mad at Isabel for trying to help. "I guess not. It tickles, though."

Isabel smiled. "Sometimes I just do it without

thinking about it. You take it better than Marisol, and she needs calming more than anyone."

Leo looked over her shoulder. The kitchen was empty. "Why doesn't Marisol like magic?"

Isabel reached for another cookie, took a bite, chewed. "Marisol . . . don't tell her I said this, okay? I think she does like magic. I think she likes it, but it scares her, so she pretends not to like it."

"Why does it scare her?"

"Oh, you know." Isabel picked crumbs off the table with her fingertip. "Marisol is scared of everything."

This didn't sound like the Marisol Leo knew. Marisol wasn't afraid of spiders or cockroaches or strangers or boys. Leo didn't know anyone so fearless.

"But there isn't anything to be scared of, right? Magic isn't *dangerous*." Leo didn't want to involve Caroline in something risky. She didn't even want anything bad to happen to Brent, not really.

"Well, sometimes a spell can backfire," Isabel said, staring down at her hands. "I guess there is some risk involved, just like with anything. Using the big ovens can be dangerous, but we practice and train so we know how to handle them safely, just like our powers. Don't worry, Leo. You'll always have your family supporting you."

Isabel probably wasn't trying to make Leo feel guilty, but her words only made Leo cringe. "Right," she muttered. "So it's true that magic experiments can go horribly wrong?"

"Oh, Marisol said something to you, didn't she? Some dire prediction of doom? Of course. I could smack her. She shouldn't be putting fears into your head just because she's afraid to do any spells."

Leo wasn't trying to make her sisters fight—they did enough of that on their own. "No, she just . . . Magic can be amazing too, right?"

Isabel beamed. "It always is. Leo, you're part of the family. You're a bruja. You don't need to be afraid of magic. It's part of you."

Leo nodded, but even with Isabel's calming magic, she still felt anxious. She had never thought her magic would hurt her—it was her friends she was worried about.

CHAPTER 16
PATIENCE

When Brent didn't show up to school on Thursday, Leo thought she might scream. She and Caroline stared at Brent's locker, but since Leo's magic did not seem to include x-ray vision, there was no way to tell if the locker had been opened or if the cookies were still there.

At lunch, Leo found herself surrounded by classmates who had questions about the snack club. Most people needed help figuring out what to bring in, but some had baking questions too.

"What does it mean when the recipe says to separate the egg?" Mary Gradel asked. "Is that the same as cracking it?"

"My mom won't let me use the oven," Lara Sanchez said. "How long do you microwave cookie dough?"

Greg Lewis ran over to the table to ask Leo, first, if boys were allowed into the snack club, and, second, what t-s-p and t-b-s-p stood for in a recipe. Leo thought that everyone in the world knew the abbreviations for teaspoon and tablespoon, but she quickly discovered that lots of the things she thought of as basic knowledge made her a sixth-grade baking expert.

"Leo is an egg-cracking *machine*." Caroline bragged. "And her kitchen has a hundred kinds of flour, and every spice you've ever heard of." The other sixth graders crowded closer with more questions, and Leo didn't know what to do with them all. The noise and excitement overwhelmed her until the bell finally rang and she could retreat back to her desk in Ms. Wood's classroom.

"I can't believe snack club is going to be a real thing," she told Caroline on the bus ride home, staring up the aisle at the profiles of kids who were turning to smile at her. "Nobody was ever interested in baking before now."

"I'm sure they were interested. Who doesn't love cookies?"

Nobody ever talked to me about it, Leo thought—but then, she had never really talked to her classmates about baking, either.

The phone rang later that evening, when Leo sat on the floor of the living room doing her homework.

"Leo," Mamá called out. "It's for you." Her and Daddy's hands were full stretching out the crust of the pizza they were making for dinner.

"Um, hello?" She rubbed the bumpy impressions the carpet had left on her elbow as she held the phone to her ear. "Caroline?"

"It worked!"

"What?"

Caroline's voice was high and thin, but Leo wasn't sure if that was excitement or phone static. "Brent ate the cookies!"

Leo glanced at Isabel, who stood a few feet away, smiling her "isn't the baby growing up so fast?" smile. Very slowly, making sure to keep her face casually blank, Leo paced away from her sister and toward the hall.

"Mm-hm." She made extra sure not to sound interested.

"Did you hear me? He ate them! I saw it through the kitchen window."

"Really?" Leo whispered while racing down the hall. "Hmm . . ."

"Leo! Are you even listening?"

Leo made it to the safety of her room and slammed the door behind her. She jumped onto her bed and kicked her feet in the air in silent triumph.

"Sorry," she whispered. "My sister was right there. Are you sure? How did you see? Tell me everything."

"I was cleaning the kitchen because I wanted to try baking in my house, you know? And Dad said that he wants to learn with me, as long as we make sure not to set anything on fire."

"That's great. I can help you both."

"Yes please! So I was standing by the window, and you know how I can see Brent's kitchen from there? He opened his backpack and took out his math book, and the cookies fell out with the book, and he looked at them and then he showed them to his mom and then he ate them. He actually ate them!"

Leo leaned back on the bed and pressed the phone against her ear, grinning hugely. "What did his mom say?"

"I couldn't hear her," Caroline reminded Leo. "She laughed, I think. How long until the spell kicks in?"

Leo hadn't thought about that. "When did he eat the cookies?"

"About two minutes ago."

"Hmm . . ." Leo had no idea how long a spell like this took to work, but she didn't want to tell Caroline that. "Well, the recipe said one bite, so it probably won't take too long. Probably you'll hear from him in an hour, since you live so close."

"You really think so?" Caroline's voice jumped even higher. "It's going to work?"

"Definitely." Leo traced the stitching on her comforter and wondered if she believed herself. "By tomorrow morning at the very latest, Brent will be begging you to be friends again."

CHAPTER 17
LOVE LETTERS

But if Brent had made up with Caroline, there was no sign of it on her face as she got on the bus the next morning. Leo watched her friend walk alone down the aisle and slink into the bus seat.

"Nothing?" Leo asked.

"Nothing." Caroline sighed, chewing on her thumbnail. "And he didn't come to the bus stop today."

"Maybe he's sick again?" Leo felt her stomach flip over itself. Her cookies couldn't make anyone sick, could they?

"I don't know." Caroline moved on to bite the

nail of her index finger.

"It's okay," Leo said as firmly as she could. "Everything's just fine. Maybe he had a doctor's appointment or had to go to school early. Don't worry about it."

Caroline nodded but continued chewing her nails.

The main hall of Rose Hill Middle School was noisiest the five minutes before homeroom started. Leo dodged between a group of slow-moving eighth graders and grabbed her locker like a drowning animal clinging to a branch to keep from being pulled downstream. Leo's locker was number 15A, the same bright red as all the lockers in the hall, with gray, white, and black paint showing underneath the scratches. Leo spun the combination lock, pulled the door toward her, and reached for the math book she would need for the beginning of the day.

She didn't expect anything to fall out of her locker, but something did.

She didn't expect the thing that fell to be an unfamiliar square of bright-pink construction paper, but it was.

And she definitely, definitely, definitely didn't expect what was written on the paper in wobbly script, with the r's erased and rewritten.

Dearest Leo,
  Always quiet, always cool,
  Always on your own at school.
  Lots of sisters, lots of cake.
  How I hope someday you'll bake
  Something wonderful for me.
  I don't even care if it's gluten free!
  Please be mine! Xoxoxoxo,
                      Brent

Leo read the note three times over, and then she dropped it on the floor and stomped on it, and then—slowly—she bent down and picked it up to read a fourth time. Her stomach churned, and her face felt hot enough to broil. Dearest? Xoxoxoxo? The love bite cookies lived up to their name and more—Brent was totally in love! But with Leo? That wasn't right. He was supposed to make up with Caroline. If he fell in love with anyone, it should have been her. Leo double checked the note, but it was still her name on top. Had she accidentally put her eyelash into the dough? Did Brent automatically fall in love with the bruja who cast the spell?

Or . . . Leo buried her red face in her locker. Had the spell not worked right?

"I have to tell you something." Leo grabbed Caroline's arm before she could sit in her regular seat at the front of the room. There was still a minute, maybe a minute and a half, until the tardy bell rang, so Leo tugged Caroline, backpack and all, out into the hallway. "I'm so sorry, Caroline, I don't know how it happened, but—"

"Look!" Caroline's eyes bulged wide and the corner of her mouth quirked up into a worried smile. "Leo, I think the spell worked a little differently than we expected. . . ."

In her hands, she held a square of bright construction paper with shaky cursive writing covering it.

Leo's mouth fell open.

Tricia and Mai rushed into class but stopped when they saw Caroline and her note.

"Oh," Mai said, "you got one too?"

"I heard he got his mom to drive him to school early just to give them all out." Tricia sighed. "Is this what it's like to become a teenager?"

Both she and Mai held their own pink squares, and Leo drew hers out of her pocket, and Caroline's smile flickered and died as she looked at the four identical-looking love letters from Brent Bayman.

Dearest Caroline,
    I love your smile,
    I love your hair.
    I'd love to see you anywhere.
    I love your brain,
    I love your house.
    You're as cute as a tiny mouse.
    Please, oh, please say you'll be mine.
    I can't even wait for Valentine's!
                        Love,
                        Brent

Dearest Tricia,
    You're as pretty as a deer,
    And I think you're really cool.
    So I hope you won't think I'm weird
    If I ask you to go out after school.
    Please say yes, I'll be so glad.
    We can eat some ice cream, maybe.
    I'll be really really sad
    If you say you won't be my baby.
                        Love,
                        Brent

Dearest Mai,
   Japanese haikus
   Are pretty and I like them
   Just like I like you.

                    Love,
                    Brent

"I'm Vietnamese!" Mai wailed, crumpling the note with a scowl after Leo had read it. "Is this some kind of joke?"

Leo looked down, suddenly feeling like the world's smallest cucaracha. She wanted to crumple her paper too. Brent hadn't even bothered coming up with different rhymes, reusing "cool" and "school" in both her poem and Tricia's. The love letter was the opposite of special, and Leo felt silly silly silly about the tiniest second when she had felt special, thinking that Brent had written it just for her.

And if that hurt her, she couldn't imagine how Caroline must feel.

"I don't know if it's a joke or what," Leo lied. "But obviously he doesn't really mean all of them. Let's just ignore it."

Tricia and Mai nodded, and Caroline joined them a few seconds later. Leo thought she saw something sparkling in Caroline's eyes, but it was hard to tell when her friend ducked behind her hair.

"Come on." Leo took Caroline's arm. "Let's get to class."

On the way to her desk, Leo saw pink construction paper squares on desks, peeking out of backpacks, and several folded up and dropped in the recycling bin. It seemed like most of the girls in the class had gotten one, and a bunch of the boys too.

And there, sitting at his desk in the center of the room, his eyes flickering from seat to seat and a dopey grin stretching his face into a dazed expression, was Brent. He met Leo's glare and beamed at her.

"Good morning, Leo. You're looking lovely today." And he gave her a terrible, horrible, mushy-gushy wink.

Leo pressed her hand to her mouth and swallowed hard to keep her Cinnamon Toast Crunch in her stomach where it belonged. She needed to do some magical damage control—fast!

CHAPTER 18
ROMANCE

Caroline did not show up in the cafeteria at lunch-time.

"Is she okay?" Mai lowered her voice so the rest of the table couldn't hear. The sixth graders buzzed about the love letters, whispering and giggling and shooting angry or confused or flirtatious looks at each other. "I don't know what's the matter with Brent, but . . . well, it did sort of seem like maybe Caroline might have liked him." Tricia nodded and leaned across the table to listen.

Leo opened her mouth, then shut it again. She had suspected the same thing, but she didn't want to add to the rumors, especially when nobody else knew the real magical cause of all the commotion. Besides, Caroline had only said she wanted to be friends with Brent again.

"I think the note surprised her." Leo shrugged. "She didn't know that everyone got one at first. I didn't either, actually. So that made it extra confusing."

Tricia and Mai nodded, pursing their lips in sympathy. "We met at our lockers, so we found them at the same time," Tricia said. "What do you think everyone's going to do?"

Leo looked over at Brent, who sat at the very end of his usual table all by himself, wearing a dreamy smile and pausing from slurping his instant noodles to scribble something in his open notebook. More love letters? Leo's stomach churned.

"I don't know . . . ," she started to say, but the question was abruptly answered when Emily Eccles threw down her uneaten granola bar, stood up, and stalked across the cafeteria to the far end of the boys' table.

"Hi, Brent." Her voice carried in the echo-y room, especially since every other middle schooler—even the eighth graders—had gone silent. Mr. Kuo, the lunch monitor for the day, looked up.

"Emily!" Brent jumped to his feet and threw his arms wide. "Emily Eccles, with the beautiful freckles, what brings you here on this fine day?"

Emily's eyes popped like a squeezed bullfrog. Leo was sure that her own face looked just the same. Brent sounded like his brain had been replaced by an alien's.

"I just wanted to ask you," she said, taking a step back from Brent's open arms but quickly recovering her smile, "if you wanted to see a movie with me this weekend." She settled into a flirty lean against the table. "Since you like my freckles so much."

Leo's table erupted in whispers. What was Emily doing? What would Brent say? Were there even any good movies playing this week?

Leo wished they would all hush. She had to see what the spell made Brent say next.

"Nothing would make me happier than to spend an evening by your side." Brent reached out to grab hold of Emily's hand. Leo's table gasped. Brent's friends, who had been trying very hard to pretend they weren't watching, gasped. The seventh and eighth graders snickered. Mr. Kuo put down his coffee and pushed his chair back, hovering hesitantly as he watched the scene play out.

Emily turned straight to her friends at Leo's table

and shot them a satisfied smirk.

"So you like *me*?" she asked Brent. "You want to be *my* boyfriend?"

Leo held her breath with the rest of the cafeteria, suddenly very glad that Caroline had not come to lunch.

"Of course!" Brent cried, pulling Emily's hand to his heart. "I love you more than anything in the world, Emily Eccles."

He sounded like a knight from a romance movie. Leo shrank in her seat, sure that someone would suspect supernatural interference any minute.

Emily freed her hand and sat in the space next to the one Brent had left. He quickly reclaimed his seat and her hand, and then started writing in his notebook again. The other boys at the table pretended to vomit. Mr. Kuo sat all the way back down, a smile on his face. Whispers flew like spinning knives from Emily's friends.

"What are you writing?" Emily asked Brent, her voice still loud, not ready to let the cafeteria return to normal just yet. She had found her spotlight, and she wasn't going to give it up until she had to.

"Oh, do you want to see? It's a love poem. For María Villarreal."

"What?" Emily snatched her hand away. Leo

buried her face in her hands, but she could still hear the whispers repeating María's name over and over. "Why are you writing a poem for her?"

"Because I love her," Brent said cheerfully.

Leo didn't need to look up to imagine the bright red of Emily's cheeks or the bounce of her curls as she tossed her head angrily, but she looked anyway, peeking through her fingers like it was a horror movie.

"You can't love María." Emily stood up again. The entire cafeteria was murmuring. Mr. Kuo stood up all the way this time, but Emily and Brent didn't seem to notice.

"But I do love her." Brent's face was still plastered with a dreamy smile. "More than anything in the world."

Emily stamped her foot. "You can't love us *both* more than anything in the world. You have to make up your mind!"

"Make up my mind? How? I love everyone in the world more than anything in the world!" Brent flung his arms wide and beamed around the cafeteria. Shocked whispers and snickers erupted from every table. Mr. Kuo started to stomp his way over to the bickering couple.

"You are a liar, Brent Bayman, and I hate you.

We are breaking up!" It was then that Mr. Kuo politely suggested that both she and Brent might want to go chat with Vice Principal Torres about the commotion. Brent gazed fondly at the cafeteria monitor, smiling and nodding as he talked.

After they left, the conversation in the cafeteria grew to a roar. María talked loudly at anyone who would listen, explaining that she was *not* interested in Brent. Following her lead, María's friends rushed to proclaim that Brent was not even that cute, anyway, and annoying to boot. Leo's stomach crawled with the horrible feeling that had been building since she had seen the first four love letters.

Something was horribly wrong with the cookies, Brent had gone totally lovesick, and it was all Leo's fault. She swallowed and coughed to clear the nervous lump in her throat, and looked at Tricia and Mai.

"Can we all agree not to tell Caroline about this?" she asked.

The two girls nodded.

Leo didn't find Caroline until class started again, and by then Ms. Wood had heard about the lunchtime theatrics and decided on silent reading and worksheet time to keep everything calm for the rest of the day. Leo spent the time not doing her language arts, but trying to formulate a plan that would fix Brent. She had made this mess, so she had to clean it up. Besides, she couldn't leave Brent the way he was. The sixth grade would tear him to pieces by the end of the week.

Why wasn't there a spell-reversal spell? Leo flipped through the pages of the recipe book for the third time, but it was no use. She'd already searched through all the recipes she could read on her own, and none of them was the slightest bit of use for stopping a magically romantic serial poet. She needed Caroline to help her read the rest of the recipes and make sense of what each spell could do . . . if Caroline would even talk to Leo after the mess she'd made of everything.

Leo tried to catch Caroline's eye for the rest of the day, but her friend kept her head buried in a book with a medieval castle on the cover, silently reading— or at least pretending to. When Leo got on the bus that afternoon, she didn't quite believe she still had a seat buddy until Caroline actually sat down.

"Hi." Leo swallowed three times, her throat suddenly dry. "Are, um, are you—you know it's just a messed-up spell, right?"

"I know." Caroline didn't meet Leo's eyes. "I just

don't understand. . . . What happened? I thought—for a second I thought he maybe *liked* me, and that was weird enough. But now I'm just confused."

"I think . . ." Leo gulped again. "I think I maybe messed things up. Please don't be mad, but . . . I think it was my fault. I think my idea worked out all wrong."

"Your idea?" Caroline met Leo's eyes, and then she gasped. "The blank part of the spell! Not making him like me. It made him like everyone."

"I'm so sorry, Caroline. I ruined everything."

"Poor Brent," Caroline whispered. "Emily Eccles is going to socially destroy him."

Leo cringed. Even though her classmates couldn't talk about anything else, she had still hoped that Caroline didn't know about the lunchtime fiasco.

"So what are we going to do about it?"

The bus turned onto Caroline's street, and Leo made a quick decision. "You're going to let me use your phone to tell my dad that I missed the bus and walked to your house, and I need a ride home. And while we're waiting, we're going to find a way to make this right."

Daddy was not happy with Leo after her phone call. He was busy filling out important paperwork for the bakery and couldn't pick her up for at least an hour, which was even more time than Leo had been counting on. She said hello to Caroline's dad, listened to Caroline's lie about a history project, and then followed Caroline down the hall into the pink-and-yellow butterfly room.

"I couldn't find a reversal spell, but maybe I missed it. I don't know the word for reverse in Spanish."

"I'll look." Caroline waited for Leo to pull out the recipe book and then started flipping the pages quickly and silently, chewing on her thumbnail.

Leo watched for a few minutes, then turned away, feeling useless. She scanned the bookshelf next to Caroline's bed, finding a few books she recognized and many more she didn't. Maybe Caroline would reopen her lending library. If they were still best friends after this, that is. Leo's shoulders slumped. Friends were different from sisters, because no matter how angry you made your sisters, they would always be your sisters.

"I just don't see anything that reverses a spell." Caroline flipped quickly through the last few pages of the recipe book. "There are no My Mistake Meltaways or Oops-a-Daisy Pies. There's not even a Forgetfulness Flan. There are about seventeen different love spells in here, but not one spell to get rid of them." She slammed the book closed, blowing hair out of her face in annoyance. "What are we going to do, Leo? We can't just leave him like this."

Leo gulped. "Maybe the spell will wear off on its own?" Her voice wasn't confident enough to fool anyone, even herself.

Caroline bit her thumbnail and tapped her foot against the floor. "You should tell your mom."

"What?" Leo pulled the spell book toward her chest. "No, I can't."

"Isabel, then," Caroline offered. "We need help."

"I can't tell them. I'm not even supposed to be doing magic. And I don't need them. I can figure this out."

Caroline stayed quiet, but the way she frowned showed she wasn't convinced. Leo hugged the spell book to her chest, as if she could squeeze a solution out of it. Caroline didn't understand—if Leo ran to Mamá or Isabel now, it would mean she really was a baby, like they all thought.

She stared hard at one of the paintings Caroline's dad had made, a purple flower smiling in the middle of a dark-gray rainstorm. "If we can't reverse the spell . . . ," she said, still thinking as she talked, "maybe we can cover it up somehow." She thought about how the thick purple spread on top of the gray paint, hiding the original color. Could spells work the same way? "How many love spells did you say were in the book?"

"I was exaggerating," Caroline admitted. "But there are at least seven. Why?"

"Because I have another idea." Leo bit her lip and put the spell book back on the bed. "I'm not really sure if it will work. But I think it's at least worth a try."

Caroline hesitated. "And it involves more magic?"

"I think another spell is the only way to stop this one." Leo shrugged. "And . . . we have to try something." She could have pretended to be more confident, but she was tired of trying to fool Caroline, especially now that Caroline already knew that Leo wasn't the world's most perfect witch. "What do you think?"

Caroline looked from Leo to the book. "What are the chances that your plan will make everything worse?"

"I have no idea," Leo answered honestly.

Caroline's nervous frown curled into a nervous smile. "Well, at least let me hear it, then."

Leo tried not to look too happy when Daddy knocked on the door, but it was hard to keep the skip out of her step as she followed him to their pickup. In her backpack was a sheet of notebook paper with a translated recipe for a love potion that was simple and sweet, just the thing to help Brent focus and stop his widespreading love fever. While Daddy lectured Leo about the inconvenience she had caused and reminded her that taking the bus home was her responsibility as part of the family, Leo just stared out the window, working out her plan to save the day.

Daddy noticed that his scolding wasn't making an impact, because he sighed and turned on the radio, and Leo watched Rose Hill fly by to the twangy voices of country singers and their equally twangy guitars. They didn't need to sound so depressed, Leo thought. If it was heartbreak they were singing about, she could have helped them out. This love thing might have some ups and downs, but she was pretty sure it always turned out right in the end.

CHAPTER 19
SPIDERWEBS

Leo felt relieved it was the weekend, because that meant no school, and no school meant no Brent. With her new spell in mind, Leo tagged along to the bakery with Isabel on Saturday morning, telling Mamá that she wanted to start helping out more now that she had practiced some baking at home. Guilt from all her lies grew bigger and bigger, like rising dough in her stomach, but she didn't have a choice if she wanted to fix her mistake.

Mamá and Isabel served customers in the front, leaving Tía Paloma in the kitchen kneading sweet-bread dough on the wooden countertop and muttering angrily to herself. Leo snuck behind her easily and made straight for the row of wooden cabinets. She needed a few special ingredients for her new spell, and she suspected that these cabinets were just the place to find them.

FRASCO DE MIEL ATRAPACORAZONES
UNA TRAMPA DE AMOR

INGREDIENTES

1 frasco de vidrio de cualquier tamaño
1 vela (para purificación)
miel, suficiente para llenar el frasco
1 telaraña
1 puñado de corazones de caramelo
unas hojas de lila

The Heart Snare Honey Jar recipe, used to attract and trap someone's mushy-gushy feelings, was simpler than the love bites. It didn't require any baking, or boiled sweatshirts or eyelashes or anything too hard to get from Brent. But it did need a single spiderweb and a box of Valentine's Day conversation hearts, which Leo didn't think they sold at the drugstore in November.

Leo started by opening the first cabinet and

quickly scanning the contents of its shelves. It was filled mostly with nonfood things—bowls and spatulas and eggbeaters and waxed paper. And on the top shelf, next to a few glass casserole dishes, Leo spotted the third thing she needed: a big glass jar with a metal lid, exactly the sort of jar that jelly or pickles might come in.

Leo glanced over her shoulder, made sure that Tía Paloma was busy. Then she stood on her tiptoes and grabbed the glass jar, pulling it down and slipping it into her backpack as quietly as she could.

She moved on to the second cabinet. The chalky conversation-heart candy was easy to find, filling a big Ziploc bag next to a smaller bag of candy corn, another filled with red-striped peppermints, and the plastic mesh sack of chocolate coins. Leo had no trouble sneaking a handful of hearts out of the bag and into her pocket (she didn't think a little bit of lint would bother the spell). *So far, so good,* Leo thought.

The spiderweb turned out to be a little trickier.

Leo scoured the corners of the bakery floor, but other than scattered specks of dust and flour, she didn't find anything. Mamá would never let spiders live in the bakery, and she would never allow dusty cobwebs to collect anywhere near the food she served her customers. Leo thought hard. She couldn't imagine Mamá putting spiderwebs from the floor into any recipe, no matter how magical. But if she didn't get her ingredients from the floor, then she must get them from somewhere. . . .

She turned back to the last cabinet, the one she hadn't looked through yet. At first glance she only saw flour, sugar, and other large bags full of common ingredients. But the top shelf, up so high Leo could barely see it, held small boxes and tins that Leo couldn't name, ingredients that she had never seen used.

A plastic bag sat on the top shelf, a gold twist tie around its neck, holding what looked like a stack of very fine lace doilies. It was next to a jar of blue-black feathers and a rolled-up paper bag labeled *Extra Strength*, along with some odd-looking dried plants and leaves that practically screamed, "Magic ingredients stored here!"

Leo checked over her shoulder. She stood on her tiptoes to get a better view of the top shelf and almost clapped her hands when she saw the title *Spider-webs* written in Tía Paloma's scratchy handwriting across the front of the plastic bag. She reached up to snatch it and—

"Is that you, Leo?" Tía Paloma asked. "Do you

happen to see where I put the bottle of vanilla extract?"

Leo startled and drew her hand back, almost knocking over the jar of feathers and accidentally pushing several of the bags into each other. The bag with the spiderwebs flopped over backward, and Leo could no longer see where it was on the shelf.

Tía Paloma bustled up behind Leo and pushed her aside to grasp a small glass vial from the middle shelf.

"Morning." Leo turned so her aunt couldn't see the lump in her backpack. "What are you making?"

Tía Paloma turned to look over her shoulder, stared into space, and didn't answer. "It's chaos around here," she said after a minute. "I would lose my head if it wasn't attached."

Leo retreated through the swinging doors, her guilt burning holes in her cheeks and through her belly button, hoping the stolen jar didn't rattle too loudly in her backpack.

In the front of the bakery, Mamá set Leo to work packing bags with gingersnaps, just like Leo and Caroline had for Brent. Leo was glad the bakery would be selling them, because that meant if Brent ever tried to investigate his secret admirer, he would find out that anyone could have bought the cookies and left them in his locker.

Not that Brent was in any condition to play detective. He was too busy composing love poems to the whole world.

As Leo filled bags and twisted the golden wires tight around them, her mind went back to the top shelf of the third cabinet. She needed those spiderwebs to make the honey-jar spell, and she needed the honey-jar spell—the heart snare—to trap Brent's wild romantic feelings until they turned back to normal.

When Leo first explained the plan, her idea to use another love spell to cover up the first, Caroline had been skeptical.

"How do we know it won't make him worse? What if the spells don't cancel each other out?"

Leo didn't have much of an answer to that. The best she could say was that the trapping part of the spell seemed right to her—it seemed like it would work for what they wanted it to do. And, she told Caroline again, Brent was already the victim of a bungled love spell. It couldn't get much worse.

Leo watched from a corner behind the counter as a family with a tiny baby came into the bakery, smiling as they placed a birthday-cake order. The silver bell on the door shook as they left. Next came a very old man who asked Isabel for his usual and was rewarded with a guava cono and a small paper cup of milk. People walked in hungry and excited, sniffing the air and greeting Mamá and Isabel and Leo with friendly waves. They left with smiles on their faces and sweetness on their tongues. Leo wanted to relax into her work and the warm bakery air. She just needed to get the spiderwebs first.

Leo shoved the rest of her twist ties into her pocket when no one was looking. Then she stood up, stretched, and walked through the swinging doors into the back of the bakery. Tía Paloma kneaded dough with her back to Leo, nodding occasionally.

"It's thick enough," Tía Paloma whispered as Leo crept across the kitchen. "Because I'm the one touching it, that's how." She sighed and then continued in an even quieter voice. "Don't you have other grandchildren to spy on?"

Leo crept to the last cabinet, hoping the ghost Tía Paloma was speaking to wasn't a tattletale. She pulled the door open. She slowly unzipped her backpack, stood on her tiptoes, and reached for the top shelf, groping for the crinkly bag with the golden twist tie. Her hand passed over the paper bag, the jar of feathers, and a lump wrapped in silky cloth before finally touching the bag of spiderwebs.

Behind her, something heavy clanged and clattered, and Tía Paloma yelped. In a flurry of panic, Leo swept everything off the shelf into her arm and shoved it into her backpack, slamming the cabinet door and turning around just in time to see Isabel run through the door and help Tía Paloma clean up the mess of the fallen tray.

Tía Paloma laughed and apologized for her clumsiness. Leo helped pick up and throw away all the lumps of unbaked dough that were now stuck to the tile floor, and nobody asked what she was doing in the back of the bakery. Nobody mentioned that her backpack was only half zipped, and fuller than it had been that morning. And as she walked carefully back to the kitchen, nobody noticed the tiny clinking noise that came from two glass jars—one empty, one full of feathers—knocking together in Leo's backpack.

The spell was officially ready to cast.

CHAPTER 20
HONEY JAR

On Monday morning, Leo got permission to go to Caroline's house after school.

"Perfect," Mamá said. "I have a special order to work on, and Daddy needs to take inventory, and we didn't want you to come home to an empty house. Have a good time, 'jita, and we'll call when we're ready to pick you up."

Brent spent the day in the same lovesick haze as before. If anything, the weekend seemed to have made him worse. He tried to serenade three different kids at lunch, but the entire sixth-grade class was giving Brent the silent treatment. He earned a detention from Ms. Wood after he proposed to Sarah Florence, one knee and all, in the middle of silent reading. "What is going on with you?" Ms. Wood demanded. Leo slouched in her seat while her stomach twisted in knots.

On the bus ride home, Brent had some trouble choosing a seat—he wanted to sit by everyone, and no one wanted to sit by him. But Mrs. Lillis glared until Brent settled next to a third-grade boy who scooted as far away as he could and stared out the window.

The girls discovered Caroline's dad unpacking boxes in the kitchen when they arrived.

"There she is!" He pulled his long legs out of the doorway and stood with only a little bit of groaning. "Leo, always nice to have you. You know, you've inspired me to make this place livable again." He gestured around the kitchen, which Leo was happy to see now included some dishes that weren't made of paper and even a small frying pan. No table yet, but it was a nice start.

Unfortunately, it was also inconvenient. The plan had been to use the kitchen for spell work, but they could hardly concoct a cover-up love spell right in front of Caroline's dad.

"Are you girls going to bake today?" Mr. Campbell

asked. "I could help out if you need something stirred or measured. Anything more complicated than that, and I'll just have to watch and learn."

Leo glanced at Caroline, who laughed nervously. "No, Dad, we're just going to do some homework in my room. Although . . ." Caroline looked at Leo for a moment, then looked back at the floor. "I think maybe we can make some tea to help us concentrate. Do you like tea, Leo? We have *honey*."

Leo worried that Caroline's eyebrows might crawl right off her face if she kept raising them like that. "I'd love some tea!"

Once they were safely locked in Caroline's room with rainbow-handled tea mugs and a bear-shaped bottle of honey, Leo unzipped her backpack to pull out the recipe book, the empty jar, the bag of spiderwebs and the pocketful of candy hearts, and a tall white candle borrowed from the dining-room drawer. The rest of the mysterious magical items she had accidentally stolen were safely stashed under her bed until she could sneak them back to the bakery. Caroline looked at the ingredients— especially the delicate spiderwebs—with awe, and listened raptly while Leo told the story of how she had almost been caught stealing them. The girls checked the recipe one more time, nodded at each other, and began the spell.

Leo started by blowing into the empty jar. She made Caroline blow into it too, since the recipe book said that all the spell workers should. Caroline argued that she was no spell worker, but Leo said that if she was going to be helping, then she counted. After they filled the jar with their breath, Leo propped the white candle up inside the jar and lit it with the matchbook Caroline had in her bedside table drawer, in case of power outages. As soon as the candle was lit, the fan in the middle of Caroline's ceiling stopped spinning and the light shut off.

Caroline gasped. Leo imagined that she could feel the electricity tingling out of the walls and into her fingers, but it might have just been the excitement of knowing that her magic really worked.

The girls watched as the candle burned down, purifying the jar, the spell, and their own intentions—according to the recipe. Leo counted out thirteen minutes on Caroline's purple cat-shaped alarm clock, and then she twisted the lid onto the jar and let the flame suffocate while she and Caroline whispered Brent's name three times. Then Leo opened the jar back up, put the candle aside, and peeled away one single spiderweb to lay at the bottom of the jar.

"It looks thin. Are you sure it's strong enough to trap all of it?"

Leo looked at the jar. She had a lot more spiderwebs she could add, but she was going to do this spell just exactly right, according to the recipe, without even the tiniest change. "It's fine," she said firmly. "What's next?"

Next was the honey bottle, which Leo emptied into the jar while concentrating on her memories of Brent's sappy notes, his cafeteria fight with Emily, and his silly serenades. These were the emotions they wanted to trap, and Leo reeled in all the sourness they had brought and replaced it with the sweetness of the honey and the candy hearts she dropped into the jar.

It was complicated, trying to think and feel and concentrate on so many things at once. But the complications made her feel strong. She could smell the magic dripping and oozing into the jar along with the honey.

When the jar was half full and the bottle almost empty, Leo stopped. She put the bottle down, licked the sticky smudges off her fingers, and brushed loose pieces of hair off her forehead.

"Next is the lilac leaves?" She looked at Caroline sitting cross-legged on the bed and watching with wide eyes as Leo worked her magic. "You said you could get that, right?"

"Got it!" Caroline reached to grab something off her bedside table. "My dad got a new bonsai collection, and one of them is a miniature lilac tree." She opened her hand, and Leo smiled at the pile of little green leaves her friend held out.

"They really look like hearts. Tiny ones." She picked up one of the leaves and dropped it into the honey. "So cute!"

Trap Brent, Leo thought as she let more leaves fall one by one into the jar. *Don't let him act enchanted anymore. Snare his feelings.*

She hoped the spell was going to work, because she had no idea what she would do if it didn't. She had followed the recipe exactly this time—from the spiderweb to the heart candies to the leaves that, while small, were still lilac. The spell had to work.

When the honey-jar trap was set, Leo screwed the lid on tight. The lights flickered back on, and the fan resumed its buzzing hum. Caroline helped Leo pack the full jar into her backpack along with the recipe book, jumping up and down as she did so.

"Now we have to bury it." Leo pulled the heavy backpack over her shoulder and tapped her fingers against the straps. "Do you think your dad would be suspicious if we did it behind your house?"

"Not at all. Let's go."

Caroline's backyard had grown wild since the move to Houston, a sea of tall spiky grass interrupted by the tree in the back corner and the round island of the trampoline that Leo was immediately tempted to visit. Mamá hated trampolines ("Unsafe!"), but Leo loved them. They'd jumped for hours when Caroline first got it.

Beyond the trampoline, under the shade of the yard's one tree, there was a long wooden table covered with potted plants and gardening tools. Leo smiled and made her way to see Mr. Campbell's bonsai.

The miniature plants were impressive, a line of three beautifully shaped trees in shallow black pots, and four or five more wobbly-looking plants that seemed bare and incomplete, some with sections of leaves turning brown or yellow.

"The nice ones he got from a nursery. He keeps trying to make his own, but they always die."

Leo nodded. "Like my dad trying to make avocado seeds sprout."

"My . . . my mom always made fun, but she loved them too. She would read outside while my dad worked on pruning new trees."

Leo traced the trunk of a bonsai that curved in a spiral. She thought of Mamá and Daddy sitting side by side in the living room, working through a pile of papers. One of them without the other would be unbalanced, off-kilter. Leo pressed her lips together and curled one hand around her stomach.

"Sorry," Caroline said. "It's weird if I talk about my mom, right?"

"Of course not! I don't know . . . I probably don't say the right thing, but you shouldn't stop talking. Unless you don't want to talk?"

"Sometimes I don't." Caroline stared at the cloudy gray sky. "Sometimes I want to pretend like everything's normal, and she's still alive and inside the house. And sometimes I get tired of pretending. It feels good to remember. Like at the Day of the Dead festival."

Leo nodded, wishing she shared Isabel's ability to comfort by magic, or at least Mamá's nonmagical talent for listening.

"The bonsai make me think of her. There's something special about them, isn't there?" Caroline asked.

Leo grazed her fingers over the light-purple blossoms of the lilac bonsai, noticing a few bare spots in the tree's heart-shaped leaf canopy. There *was* something special about the tiny trees. She could imagine fairies living under the branches.

"Let's dig here." They had planned to bury the jar on the west side of the yard, as close as they could get to Brent's house. But looking at the bonsai trees, Leo felt certain that the plants carried their own kind of magic, and she wanted to tap into that magic. What better place to hide a spell than in a fairy garden?

"Okay." Caroline glanced at the living-room window and then positioned herself so that any of Leo's movements would be blocked from sight. "There's a little shovel behind that pot. Tell me if you need help or want to switch places."

The shade of the table discouraged the grass, making Leo's digging easier. A few scoops down, the dirt was soft and damp and dark. In almost no time at all, her nails were black rimmed, and the jar fit into the hole with only a little bit of pushing and wiggling around the sides. Leo patted the dirt down around the jar, said a quick prayer hoping for this to actually work, and then stood up and smiled at Caroline, trying to look less nervous than she felt.

"The recipe said it needs to stay overnight." Caroline glanced toward Brent's yard, then at her living-room window, then at the still slightly noticeable bulge of dug-up and replaced dirt under their feet. "So we definitely, definitely won't see results until tomorrow."

"Right, so we definitely don't need to worry about it until morning."

"Right. No worries," Caroline said.

The two girls stared at each other and worried.

"We could . . . I guess we could go lie on the trampoline, if you want."

"Yeah." But Leo didn't move, and neither did Caroline, and they both stood in front of the table worrying until Caroline's dad came outside to ask if they wanted to order pizza for dinner.

Mamá couldn't understand Leo's hurry to scarf down her scrambled eggs the next morning. Isabel and Marisol couldn't understand why she craned her neck to try to spot the school bus from blocks away. And Mrs. Lillis couldn't understand why Leo nearly sprinted up the bus steps and down the aisle, slamming into her seat.

Leo kept tapping her toes and drumming her fingers until the bus pulled up to Brent and Caroline's stop, and then she leaned forward in her seat and watched as . . . a third grader walked onto the bus, followed by Caroline, alone, chewing on her pinky fingernail and tugging her ponytail. And then the doors closed.

"I don't know," Caroline whispered before Leo could even ask anything. "I don't know if it worked. I don't know what happened. I don't know where he is!" Her voice squeaked on the last sentence, and the fifth graders in the seat in front of her turned around to giggle.

"It's okay." Leo tapped her feet faster than ever. "Maybe he just got sick again. Maybe he's cutting class. Maybe his mom is taking him to the psychiatrist to figure out what happened to his brain."

Caroline's face went white. "You don't think she really would, do you?"

"Um, no, probably not." Leo didn't want to make Caroline worry any more. "I'm sure everything's fine." And then, because she had made up her mind to try not to lie to Caroline anymore: "I hope."

Despite that hope, Leo got more and more worried as the day went on. Volunteering to bring the attendance sheet to the office, Leo saw that Ms. Wood had marked Brent's absence unexcused, which meant that his mom hadn't called. During the daily math warm-up, Leo overheard Josh and Randall talking about how mad Coach Q was going to be at Brent for missing another soccer practice without giving any notice.

Then, after lunch, Ms. Wood had red eyes and a worried expression and didn't act at all surprised when Josh, Randall, and Emily Eccles were all called to Principal Jefferson's office right in the middle of silent reading time.

Caroline turned around in her desk. Her eyes were wide and full of panic. Leo scribbled a note on a scrap of paper ripped from her notebook, dropped it on Caroline's desk on her way to pick a new book from the classroom library, and when she guessed Caroline had taken enough time to read the plan, took a deep breath and started to cough as loudly and violently as she could.

"Goodness, Leo, are you all right?" Ms. Wood pressed her bright-red nails to her mouth, looking more upset than a simple coughing fit deserved. "Why don't you go get some water?"

Just a few minutes later, Caroline joined Leo in the girls' bathroom, pulling her cell phone out of the pocket of her jeans.

"I don't know the number, but my dad taught me how to use 411." She dialed the number and held her phone to her ear. "Hello? Um, Rose Hill, Texas. Can you give me the number for Mrs. Margaret Bayman?"

Leo raised her eyebrows, impressed. She didn't

know how to look up phone numbers without the internet.

"Yes, thank you." Caroline pulled the phone away from her mouth. "She's connecting me," she whispered. "It's ringing. . . . Oh, Leo, you do it!" And she pushed the phone up to Leo's ear, just in time for a shaky voice to say, "Hello?"

"H-hello, Mrs. Bayman? Is, um, may I please speak to, um, Brent? Your son?"

Caroline had her head pressed close to Leo's, so they both jumped when a horrible strangled wailing sound came out of the phone.

"Who is this?" Mrs. Bayman's voice was frantic. "What do you want? Who are you? Do you know something about my Brent?"

Leo snatched the phone out of Caroline's hand and hung up, her heart pounding, cold panic tingling down her arms. Something was wrong. Beyond wrong—something was terrible.

"We have to go over," she told Caroline. "Right after school."

Caroline nodded mutely, her face pale and her thumbnail stubbed and bleeding.

Leo used Caroline's cell phone to call Mamá the second school let out. "I'm sorry," she said, not even caring if Mamá heard how upset she was, "I know I'm supposed to ask beforehand, but I need to go to Caroline's house today. It might be an emergency."

"Oh, 'jita," Mamá sighed. "I do wish you could have eased me into this whole growing-up thing a little slower. I'm glad you and Caroline are falling into your old routine, but I don't want you to completely disappear on us."

"Mamá . . ."

"But I remember what middle school is like. Go. Take care of your emergency. Just promise me you two will take care of some emergencies over here, sometimes."

"Okay, Mamá." Leo hung up the phone, feeling queasy and jittery like she had just eaten a whole gallon of coffee ice cream. Mamá thought that her emergency was a middle-school thing, a growing-up thing, like makeup or mean-girl drama. What would she do if she suspected the truth?

"He's okay, right?" Caroline fidgeted with her shirt. They waited anxiously for the bus to pull up in front of the school. "He has to be okay."

"It was just a love spell," Leo whispered as they climbed into their seats.

"Brent's mom overreacts," Caroline repeated to

herself over and over during the short bus ride.

They fell silent when the bus pulled up to Caroline's street and they saw the flashing blue and red lights of the police cars encircling Brent's house.

CHAPTER 21
GONE!

"Dad?" Caroline called as soon as she opened the back door.

"Caroline!" Mr. Campbell ran into the kitchen, his pale face matching his daughter's perfectly. "Oh, and Leo. Always good to have you, but . . . do your parents know you're over? They might want you home today."

Leo couldn't answer him. Her mouth was too full of bad guilty feelings.

"Dad, what's going on?" Caroline said.

"I don't want you girls to worry." Caroline's dad kept glancing toward the window, where the flashing lights glinted, "but if you know anything about—if either of you talked to Brent Bayman recently . . . he's missing."

"Missing?" The words left Leo's mouth before she decided to say them. "What do you mean, missing? How can he be missing?"

"Gone from his bed this morning. No sign of a break-in, so he must have left on his own. So if you know anything, it's very important that you tell the police," Mr. Campbell explained, his face grim.

Caroline reached for her dad's hand, then for Leo's. Leo gripped Caroline's soft fingers while her mind ran in pointless circles and collapsed on the dizzying realization: Brent was gone. Leo's legs shook and she clung tighter to Caroline's arm to stay upright.

Brent was gone, and it must be her fault. But how?

Maybe he had run away from home after all. Maybe the confusion of so many love spells had made him chase after a passing car. That had to be it—he was lost, but the police would find him. But even when Brent came home, there was no way Leo could hide her spell casting from her family now. She was going to be in so much trouble.

Leo wished she was a regular witch, the kind

from movies and TV shows who could snap a finger and make herself disappear. The kind who used her magic to fix messes, not to make them.

She hoped Brent was safe, wherever he was. She hoped he was somewhere. If only she had never tried that horrible honey jar. . . .

The honey jar.

"Caroline." Leo tugged her friend's hand, "Caroline, can we—can we go outside for a minute? I want to . . ." She didn't know how to finish, but luckily no one expected her to.

Caroline nodded, and Mr. Campbell kissed the top of his daughter's head. "If you don't mind, Leo, I'll drive you home in a little while. Caroline, you come too, okay? I'd rather not be worrying about you."

"Okay," Caroline said. "Just give us a few minutes?"

Mr. Campbell nodded. Leo and Caroline headed for the backyard as quickly as they could.

It was truly cold now, enough that Leo shivered under her sweater. The bonsai still stood on the wooden table, and the ground under the table still bulged slightly from yesterday's digging.

"We have to dig it up. And destroy it."

"Will that help?"

Leo didn't bother to lie. "I don't know."

The two girls paid no attention to secrecy this time. They clawed up chunks of loose dirt desperately, revealing the shiny golden lid of the jar in just a few seconds. It took longer to dig around the jar, to create enough space to lift it out of the ground. It was heavy, Leo thought as she pulled it into her lap and brushed caked dirt off the sides. She didn't remember it being so—

Caroline squeaked.

Inside the jar was a person. A tiny person, no more than five inches tall, but a person unmistakably. The person was curled up and suspended in the honey, eyes closed and hands folded as if he were enjoying a nice nap. The person even wore Spider-Man pajamas.

The person, unless Leo's eyes were playing tricks on her, was Brent Bayman.

"Leo . . ."

"Girls," Mr. Campbell called from inside.

"I'll call you tonight," Leo said, shoving the jar into her backpack, dirt and all. "I'll find a way to fix it. I'll—" She gulped, struggling to zip her backpack with a shaking hand. "I'll get help. I'll figure it out. I promise."

CHAPTER 22
OUT OF THE JAR

Leo thanked Mr. Campbell for the ride but didn't invite him or Caroline in. She didn't think Mamá and Daddy had heard about Brent, and she didn't want them to, yet. She needed time to think.

Mamá was busy on the phone, and Isabel and Marisol fought over a pair of tights that Marisol had "borrowed" and then ripped, so Leo only had to return a wave and ignore a questioning look, and then she was free to dart into her room and close the door.

She put her backpack on her bed and stared at it as though it might burst into flames at any moment.

She wished Caroline could have stayed.

Leo unzipped the backpack and gently lifted out the honey jar. Tiny Brent still slept inside. Leo stared in horror and fascination, watching tiny bubbles float out of Brent's open mouth. She watched his minuscule eyelashes twitch.

Finally, like jumping off a diving board, Leo squeezed her eyes shut and twisted the lid.

Pop! The jar snapped open and the lid wrenched out of Leo's hand and flew a foot into the air. Tiny Brent also flew, luckily not so high that Leo couldn't hold out her hand and catch him.

"Ah!" Brent's voice was only a little squeakier and quieter than normal, which meant that his scream was still very loud. *"Aaaah!"*

"Shh!" Leo tried to cover him with her other hand, but he was too big and his legs and arms flailed wildly, getting honey all over Leo's fingers.

"Help! Mom! Aaaah!"

"Shush! Brent, be quiet." Leo lifted her hand closer to her face, and Brent snapped his mouth shut and stared wildly around the room. "Shh . . . ," Leo said again. "It's all right. It will be all right—"

"Leo?" Isabel knocked on the door. "Are you okay, sweetie?"

"Fine!" Leo called, her own voice shrill with

fright. "I was trying to reach the top of my closet and I almost fell! Hahahaha—" She put her hand over her mouth to stop the hysterical laughter spilling out and tasted honey.

"Okay," Isabel called. "Come for dinner soon. Daddy's making quesadillas."

Leo waited for the sound of her sister walking back down the hall before she took her hand away from her mouth. "Okay," she whispered. "Please keep quiet, Brent. I'm sure you're confused. . . ."

Leo didn't know where to start. While she tried to think of a way to explain things, Brent spun around in her palm, his eyes wide and mouth open as he took in the room.

"I don't . . . where . . . what's happening?" Brent looked from Leo's face to her palm under his feet. "What am I . . . ?" He turned until he found the mirror hanging above Leo's dresser. Leo met his eyes in the mirror as he took in the whole scene. She hoped he wouldn't scream again.

"You shrank me!" Brent spat, though he did keep his voice low. "You shrank me, Leo Logroño, and I'm telling my mom, and you're going to go to jail for . . . for shrinking me. And what am I covered in?"

"Hold on, look, this was all an accident. I never meant— It's just honey," Leo said.

Brent hesitated, then cautiously licked his hand. "Oh, okay." He watched the honey drip from his fingers, his face turning calm. "This isn't happening." He reached with one honey-coated hand and dug his fingernails into his honey-coated arm in a vicious-looking pinch. "Ow."

"Brent, don't . . ."

Brent faced the mirror again, waved, made faces, hopped up and down. Leo wondered if the honey had dripped into his brain.

"You're supposed to wake up if you look in the mirror during a dream," he finally explained. "You can't see yourself normally. You also can't read clocks." He nodded glumly to Leo's alarm clock. "This isn't happening, this isn't happening. Why aren't any of the normal dream tricks working?"

"Because it's not a dream."

Brent looked down at his slowly dripping pajamas. "Okay." He took a deep breath. "Well, then . . . can I use your bathroom?"

"Probably not," Leo answered honestly. At maybe five inches tall, Brent would have a hard time with the faucets. "But I can bring you some water, and a bowl, and . . . give me a second."

"Leo . . . what's going on?"

Leo had no good answer to that question. She

couldn't explain anything without revealing every-thing. Maybe it was too late to worry about secrecy, but she didn't know what to do.

"Let me get you some bathwater," she said. "It's going to be okay. Just . . . wait here." She glanced around the room and then dropped Brent on the table in front of her three-story wooden dollhouse, which was just Brent's size. "You can sit in there if you want. I'll be right back."

When Leo returned from the bathroom with Mari-sol's jewelry bowl, emptied of its contents and filled with warm water, Brent was sitting on the front steps of the dollhouse wiping honey out of his hair. "Thanks," he said when Leo set the bowl down on the counter and lifted him to climb in. "Sorry about saying you were going to jail. Whatever's happen-ing to me, it's not like it's your fault. I've just been having a really strange week." He ducked under the water and rubbed the stickiness off his face.

Leo's stomach twisted. Brent's terrible week *was* all her fault, even if he had been cruel to Caroline. Now he was confused and scared, and even though Leo's brain spun with possible lies she could tell him to keep her family's secret, she owed Brent an honest answer.

She sighed and sat down on the edge of her bed.

"Brent, do you remember the note Caroline sent you last week? And how mean you were about it?"

She told the whole story, start to finish, while Brent scrubbed honey off of his clothes and body. She took a break in the middle to switch the sweetened water for clean rinse water, and another to get Brent a washcloth to dry himself off. After she finished, Brent sat in silence for a long time. Leo tried to wait patiently—she knew it was a lot for him to hear in one sitting. She hoped he wasn't going to scream or yell again, but she couldn't blame him if he did. She fiddled with the dollhouse furniture, setting the rooms up for company.

"That," Brent finally said, "is ridiculous. There's no such thing as magic."

"What are you talking about? I gave you a love potion and it worked. And look at yourself! I shrank you."

"There must be a logical explanation. You're not a mad scientist, are you?"

"No, weren't you listening? I'm a witch!"

"Hmph." Brent wrapped himself in the washcloth, which dragged behind him like a dingy gray bridal train. "No, you're not smart enough to be a mad scientist. Caroline, maybe."

"I'm smart!" Leo cried, her cheeks turning red.

"I'm plenty smart enough to be a mad scientist, for your information. I just happen not to be one, because I'm busy being a witch."

"Hmph."

Leo was starting to think she liked the love-bitten Brent better than the regular one. "Here." She peeled a pair of red pants and a yellow T-shirt off the wire-limbed big brother doll. "Put these on and let your pajamas dry." *Before I lock you in a drawer,* she added silently.

She set up a changing room made out of two old picture books propped upright, since the dollhouse was specifically designed not to give the dolls any privacy. After a few seconds, Brent emerged from between the books, looking like a scarecrow in the baggy new clothes. "I'm hungry. Are you going to feed me while you keep me prisoner?" he said.

"I'm not keeping you prisoner. I'm helping you."

"So will you bring me home?"

"No! I can't. I'm not done helping you yet—"

"Leeee-onora!" Daddy's voice interrupted, luckily from far enough down the hall that Leo could shove the makeshift bathtub behind the dollhouse, push the picture books down flat, and grab Brent by the back of his shirt and hide him on the top floor of the dollhouse before jumping onto her bed just in time to be reading quietly when Daddy knocked and pushed the door open. "Leonora, dinner's ready. We're all waiting for you."

"Okay, Daddy. I'll be right there. Just . . . one second?"

"Sure, but hurry up. My quesadillas are in high demand, you know." He turned and headed back down the hall. "They won't last forever."

"Quesadillas?" Brent poked his head out of the top window of the dollhouse, making the puppy-dog face Leo recognized from the festival.

She sighed. "I'll bring you one. Do you like salsa?"

CHAPTER 23
EMERGENCY

At dinner, Leo did her best to blend in with the wall. Mamá's voice drifted out from the study, where she talked to Tía Paloma on the phone. Alma and Belén were "studying" for their December finals by attempting to develop their psychic twin powers, thus allowing them to each cram only half of the material—they had been silently staring at each other all evening, without any apparent success. Daddy and Marisol argued back and forth about some boring thing from the news, and Isabel tried to keep peace between them. Leo finished her meal quickly and quietly and then hid half of her second quesadilla in a napkin to carry back to her room.

"Here, eat this." Leo shoved the folded tortilla through the dollhouse window. "I'll be right back. I have to make a phone call."

"It's as big as I am!" Brent called back. Leo couldn't tell if he was complaining or celebrating. She scrambled down the hall and stopped just outside the study to see if Mamá had finished her conversation.

"Are you sure you didn't leave them somewhere, Paloma?" Mamá asked. "Did you check your sewing basket?" She paused. "The feathers too. And you're positive you didn't use them? Hmm . . . well, I just don't see the point of breaking into the bakery only to make off with a couple of ingredients, no matter how rare. I'll ask my girls. Maybe Isabel has been practicing. But really, I'll be there to help you look tomorrow. I'm sure it's not—" Mamá turned and saw Leo in the doorway.

"Leo! Hi, sweetie, what's up? Paloma, I'll have to call you back. Yes, I'll ask. No, of course I believe you. Bye, amor. Besitos." Mamá took the phone away from her ear and smiled at Leo, who was trying to scrape up any fraction of magical talent she had to transform herself into a chair or a potted plant. "Hey, 'jita, how are you? You seemed upset earlier."

Leo tried to smile, but after hearing Mamá's side of the phone conversation, her cheeks felt broken. Tía Paloma had noticed the missing ingredients— the spiderwebs and the feathers and the jars and everything—and now Mamá knew about them too! The harder Leo tried to look innocent, the more she could feel her face twisting, sweat gathering in front of her ears.

"Mamá, I wondered if . . . I need to— Can I use the phone?" Leo kept her eyes glued to the floor and wiggled her toes nervously through her green-and-purple octopus socks.

Mamá smiled. "Calling Caroline?"

Leo nodded without looking up.

"Fine, 'jita. You know, if you want to talk, I'm here. Middle school is tough sometimes, but I got all your sisters through it, gracias a Dios."

"I'm okay, really. Just homework stuff." Leo didn't remember exactly what sorts of trouble her sisters got into in middle school, but she was pretty sure it wasn't as bad as making a Thumbelina-sized boy. And none of them had ever robbed the bakery. Mamá handed Leo the phone and shouted for Isabel.

In her room, Leo dialed Caroline's phone number, the one for her cell phone that Caroline had written in Leo's notebook. It only rang once before Caroline answered. "What's happening? Tell me! Is he . . . is Brent . . . ?"

"He's . . . small," Leo said. "Really small, like you saw. But he's um, alive, and eating. And he's not serenading me, so I think that part actually worked."

Brent poked his head out the window and waved a cheese-and-pico-covered arm.

"Oh, great. That's just great, Leo," Caroline whispered angrily. "He's not in love with the sixth grade anymore, he's just five inches tall."

"I know! I'm sorry."

"This whole thing is a disaster. I can't believe I let you talk me into it." Caroline's anger seeped through the phone.

"We did it together."

"But now it's all horrible," she yelled. "You didn't say this would happen. I just . . . I can't believe you did this."

She hung up the phone. The sound of the dial tone rang in Leo's ears; tears pricked her eyes. She had definitely lost her best friend now.

She took three deep breaths. She was on her own.

"Was that my mom? Can I talk to her?" Brent called from the dollhouse.

"It wasn't . . . Why would I be calling your mom?" Leo couldn't keep the frustration out of her voice, so her words came out in a snap.

The phone rang again. She answered on the first ring so her sisters wouldn't pick up.

"Leo?" Caroline's voice sounded like a mouse's.

"Caroline, I'm sorry."

"I'm sorry too. I just—"

"I know."

Caroline sighed. "Leo, how are we going to . . . ?"

"You're talking to *Caroline*?" Brent called out.

"Yes, hush!"

"We might have to tell your mom," Caroline said.

"How is Caroline going to help with any of this?" Brent yelled.

Leo clamped her hand over her free ear and sighed in frustration. "Caroline, I'll call you back. And no, I'm not talking to my mom, or anybody's mom. I'm going to figure this out."

"But . . . but if you don't think of anything . . ." Caroline gave a shaky sigh.

"I'll call you back." She hung up before Caroline could say anything else and hid the phone under her pillow. Caroline didn't understand anything if she thought Leo could simply go to Mamá and ask for help unshrinking a boy. Leo couldn't imagine the disappointed look Mamá would unleash, or the ear-blistering lecture. No way would Mamá let her work in the bakery. She might even—Leo gulped—refuse to teach Leo any magic until she was thirty. Or fifty! Or *never*. Leo would be the only girl in the family to be unmagical and uninitiated and alone.

No, Leo couldn't let Mamá find out. She would have to find a counterspell herself. Were there even counterspells? Reverse spells? They didn't find one for the love-bite spell. And it would take Leo forever to translate her way through the spell book.

"Hey." Brent peeked out of the dollhouse, chewing on a piece of quesadilla that looked as big as a whole pizza in his hands. "You're going to call my mom soon, aren't you?"

"Why do you keep asking that?" Leo groaned. She pulled the recipe book out of her backpack and dropped it onto the desk in front of the dollhouse, flipping it open randomly to a recipe for cookies that would either cause or get rid of warts. It wasn't very helpful, but at least glancing through the pages made Leo feel like she was trying to fix the problem.

"Well, someone needs to call her," Brent said. "She's going to be so worried. She probably already is—"

Leo slammed the book shut so hard it made the dollhouse shake. Brent grabbed the side of the wall to keep from falling. Leo immediately felt even worse than before.

"I'm sorry." She put her hand on the house to settle it. "I'm sorry, I'm sorry, I'm sorry! I don't know how to fix it, and I can't tell anyone, and I *can't* call your mom."

"How would you feel if it were your mom?"

Leo would feel terrible. Leo did feel terrible. She remembered Mrs. Bayman's crying and Mr. Campbell's grim face. If Leo knew that Mamá and Daddy were suffering that much, she would do anything to call them.

"Okay, but you can't tell her anything, please. Not yet. I'm going to fix everything." She took the phone from under her pillow and picked up Brent, placing him on her knee. "What's the number?"

"Dial star sixty-seven first," Brent said, "so she can't see the caller ID."

Leo dialed, and Brent climbed onto the phone and peered down into the mouthpiece as it rang.

"Hello? Hello?" a frantic Mrs. Bayman shouted.

"Mom?" Brent shouted back.

"Baby, is that you? I can't hear you. Where are you? I'm going to come get you right now."

"Mom, I can't talk right now. I'm fine, though," he said.

"Where are you?" Her voice grew louder. "I can

barely hear you. Where have you been all day?"

"I can't tell you what's going on or where I am. It's . . . a secret. But don't worry, seriously, I'm fine. I'll see you soon."

Mrs. Bayman burst into tears. Her sobs echoed in Leo's room.

"Hang up," Brent whispered. But Leo was frozen. So Brent climbed up the phone and leaned against the red button.

"I'm so sorry. I'll fix this."

He looked up at her. "Can you?"

Leo looked at the recipe book she could barely read and thought about all the ways her magic had already messed up. She didn't know all the rules of being a witch, but the rules of being a good person meant she had to do whatever she could to fix her mistakes. Even if it meant getting into trouble. She couldn't keep hurting Brent and Caroline because she was afraid.

"I can't fix it," she admitted. "Not on my own. Wait here a minute. I'll be back."

The door to Marisol and Isabel's room was wide open, which was only the case when the two girls argued. Leo wished she had picked a day when Isabel was in a better mood to ask for help, but Mrs. Bayman's tears compelled her to step into the doorway and cough.

"Leo?" Isabel turned around. "What's up?"

Leo walked inside without saying anything. The left side of the room—Marisol's half—was in its usual state of chaos, with black tank tops and neon leggings strewn across the floor, books and papers with colorful doodles falling off the desk. Marisol sprawled on her unmade bed with her back to the door, and Leo could hear the music blasting out of her headphones from where she stood.

Isabel's side of the room was tidy and pastel, with a large color-coded whiteboard calendar hanging over the bed. Isabel sat at her desk with a book open in front of her, but an indent in her normally crisp bed and the haphazard placement of her stuffed duck, Patty, meant that she had been moping recently. Leo climbed onto the bed and pulled Patty into her lap, hoping that the duck would give her courage. "What are you doing?" she asked.

Isabel sighed before answering. "Just getting some homework done. Because I'm the responsible one. Which apparently counts for nothing around here."

Leo nodded, rubbing the worn-down bumps of Patty's yellow fur. Marisol still hadn't turned around, and Leo was pretty sure her moody sister couldn't hear anything through her music, but she still hesitated. She couldn't just blurt out that she had a boy living in her dollhouse. She had to start at the beginning. But where was the beginning of this mess?

"And you would think," Isabel continued before Leo could collect her thoughts, "that if Mamá noticed—especially on the very same day that Marisol stole *my* clothes out of *my* closet—that if Mamá noticed things missing from the bakery, she might try interrogating the family juvenile delinquent." Isabel glared across the room at Marisol's unresponsive back. "But *no*. It must be me who stole the things, because I spend so much time at the bakery and I'm so interested in learning—" Isabel stopped, glanced at the door, and added more quietly, "Learning magic. In other words, because I'm responsible." Isabel huffed one last time and then smiled a little sheepishly. "Sorry, Leo. I'm not mad at you."

Now Leo really didn't know what to say. Heart pounding, stomach twisting, she swallowed a few times. "What happened? What's missing from the bakery?"

"Some special ingredients. Crow feathers and spiderwebs and a few other things. Marisol says it wasn't her, but I don't really see Alma and Belén getting up to that sort of thing—they have enough trouble learning to control their ghosts. But then where . . . ?"

Leo stared straight at her lap. Isabel leaned forward, trying to meet her eyes, which Leo promptly shut.

"Leo . . . ?"

Leo couldn't answer, not with Marisol sitting so near. It was one thing to come to Isabel for help—at least Isabel liked magic. Marisol had threatened to tell Mamá if she caught Leo again.

"Leo, you *didn't* . . ."

Leo didn't know what to say. She set Patty gently on the bed and grabbed Isabel's hand, towing her out the door, up the hallway, and straight to Leo's bedroom.

"I need help," Leo whispered as Isabel stepped into Leo's room.

"Leo. What did you do?"

"I have a problem, a magic problem, and I need help. It's a magic emergency." She followed Isabel inside.

"Okay," Isabel said. "At least we know what happened at the bakery. But I don't see any emergencies."

"Brent? Can you, um, come out?" It was nice of

him to hide, she thought. He didn't know who was coming in, and he could have tried to get the attention of Mamá or anyone who might call his mother. But he had hidden to keep Leo out of trouble. That was nice. Leo didn't deserve that niceness. "My sister is here to help."

Isabel whipped her head around the room, checking the closet, the space under the bed, even craning her neck to see behind the bedside table. All the places a normal sixth-grade boy might be able to hide. She didn't seem to notice the rustling coming from the dollhouse until Brent's tiny head appeared in the window and his tiny arm waved to attract her eye.

"Hi," he said. "I sure hope you're better at this magic stuff than Leo is. Also, are there any more quesadillas?"

Leo couldn't really blame Isabel for screaming.

CHAPTER 24
DUEL

Isabel recovered quickly, stamping her foot and yelling out, "Daddy, will you buy bug spray next time you go out? Leo had a roach in her room and it scared me to death!"

"Thanks a lot," Brent said, but Isabel didn't answer, just stared at him and then at Leo and then at the door. Thinking of getting Mamá? Leo hoped not.

Finally Isabel brought both hands up to her face. Leo cringed in case her sister screamed again, or cried.

"Isabel?"

"Sorry." Isabel's voice rang out high and muffled through her hands. "Sorry, I . . . Sorry." She bent forward, and Leo realized that her sister was laughing.

"Isabel! It's not funny."

"I know, I know. It's not—" Isabel tried to catch her breath but had to cover her mouth again when a giggle escaped. "It's not funny. I'm so sorry, Leo. And . . . is it Brent?"

"Brent Bayman. Nice to meet you." Brent stuck his tiny hand out the window for a shake. Isabel only laughed harder.

A scratching noise on the closed door made Leo turn around, and a second later Marisol pushed the door open, Señor Gato dashing past her into the room. Isabel, who still tried to cover her laughter, did nothing at all to block Marisol's view of the tiny person still hanging out of the dollhouse window.

"I knew it." Marisol's headphones hung around her neck, and she scowled through smudged eyeliner. She pointed her finger not at Leo, who expected it, but at Isabel. "I knew this would happen if you kept encouraging her." Marisol shut the door behind her and stomped over to the dollhouse, scooping Brent up carefully in her cupped hands and examining him. Brent tried to protest, but one icy glare from

Marisol silenced him.

Isabel had stopped laughing. "I had nothing to do with this," she snapped. "But I'm going to fix it. You can help, unless you want to hide from the big, scary magic."

Leo had no interest in her sisters' bickering. "You're going to fix it? How?"

Isabel and Marisol were too busy glaring to answer. Her oldest sister stood there until Marisol crossed the room and let Brent step onto her hand. Both girls climbed onto Leo's bed and sat cross-legged, facing each other. Isabel gently tipped Brent onto the bed between them.

Señor Gato leaped onto the bed, eyeing the tiny Brent and crouching into pounce position. Isabel and Marisol were still busy with their staring contest, so Leo pushed him off and shooed him out of her room.

"What are you doing?" Brent turned nervously to face Isabel, then Marisol. "Have your methods been tested and peer reviewed? I don't want to end up a failed experiment!"

"Hush, pipsqueak. You're fine." Marisol rolled her eyes.

"Come here, Leo." Isabel made room for Leo on the bed. Crawling up to form a triangle with Marisol and Isabel made Leo feel young, like she and her sisters could have been playing dolls or having a tea party.

"One of the reasons you shouldn't do magic before your lessons start"—Isabel raised her eyebrows in a look designed to make Leo feel guilty—"is because you won't know how to fix your mistakes."

"I looked for undo spells, but there weren't any in the recipe book. I wasn't trying to shrink him," Leo explained.

"What were you trying to do, then?" Isabel asked, but to Leo's relief, Marisol interrupted.

"I don't care what she was doing. Leo, we can fix this, but only if you promise—no more magic experiments."

"I . . ." Leo looked to Isabel, but her sister nodded. Even after all the mix-ups, Leo wasn't ready to give up and forget all about her magic for three whole years. She wanted to learn how her spells had gone wrong, and she wanted to study how to make them go right next time. She wanted there to *be* a next time, and soon.

But Leo had dragged Brent into this mess, and she had to get him out of it. And to do that, she needed her sisters' help. She sighed. "I promise."

"Yeah, I don't buy it. You already promised me

you were going to stay out of trouble, and look how well that turned out." Marisol shrugged, ruining Leo's moment of self-sacrifice.

"Excuse me, ma'am?" Brent stared up at Isabel, his hand raised like he was in school. "It's . . . it's not really magic, is it? I mean . . . magic doesn't exist . . ."

Isabel and Marisol looked at Brent, looked at Leo, looked at each other.

"Anyway," Marisol said to Isabel, "if we really want to put a stop to it, we're going to have to tell Mamá."

"Marisol! You can't!" Leo grabbed Isabel's arm. "I promise, Isabel, I won't mess with magic anymore. Don't tell Mamá!"

"Cucaracha, you lost your right to make cute puppy-dog eyes when you shrank your friend."

"Leo, stop pulling at me. Marisol, stop torturing her."

"I want her to be safe," Marisol said. "You're the one who's been filling her head with magic she's not ready for. You're the one who started all of this. I'm just trying to end it."

Isabel took a deep breath, closed her eyes. "Just hold on a minute," she said in a soft voice. Leo found herself nodding along, her panic fading as the muscles in her shoulders relaxed. She barely noticed the buzzing in her head or the way the room tilted. "Nobody wants Leo in danger— Ow!"

Isabel clapped a hand to her cheek and ducked to avoid the second toothpick Marisol flicked toward her. Leo shook her head, clearing away the dizziness and the magical calm that Isabel had created. Another toothpick appeared in Marisol's open palm and flew straight into Isabel's ponytail.

"Marisol!" Isabel snapped. "Cut that out."

"What? It's fine for you to use your magic on me, but I can't fight back?"

"I didn't *attack* you. I was just trying to— Ow! You're being so immature. You don't take any of the magic seriously, anyway, so why pretend like you care now?"

Brent turned from one sister to the other like he was watching a game of Ping-Pong. Leo tried to shrink into her bed.

"So what? I should always be experimenting and working and not having any friends? Having magic isn't about hiding from real life."

"Having magic isn't about forging hall passes and getting free makeup and avoiding responsibilities." Isabel closed her eyes, and Leo yelped as a wave of anxiety hit her, the accompanying dizziness almost knocking her off the bed.

"Turn it off," Marisol whispered through clenched teeth, "or I swear I will start throwing spiders. *Now*, Isabel."

The two girls stared at each other. Marisol held her hand palm out, like a weapon.

"S-stop," Leo said. Her sisters turned to look at her. "Stop, please, both of you. You're not—you're making everything worse." She threw her hands over her face, expecting spiders to fly at her any second.

"Sorry, Leo. I'm sorry. You're right," Isabel said with a sigh. "Neither of us just set a very good example of what being a bruja is about."

"You started it," Marisol muttered, but she held up her hands in defeat when Isabel clucked her tongue.

"Having magical abilities . . . it doesn't mean holding power over people. It's supposed to be a way to express your love. A way to take care of each other."

"But taking care doesn't always mean covering for," Marisol said with a scowl. "Not if the person you love is playing with fire." She made a fist and opened her hand to reveal a purple lighter just like the one she had used for Alma and Belén's magic ceremony, which she flicked on and off. "It's not like I want to get you in trouble, cucaracha, even if you do deserve it." She turned to Isabel, "So, last chance. If you're sure you can fix this without Mamá's help . . . then I won't say anything."

Isabel nodded. She offered Marisol a small smile. Marisol shrugged, but she didn't roll her eyes or scowl.

Isabel clapped her hands once. "Right. Now we need to get this boy normal sized and back home."

"Please," Brent added.

"Leo," Isabel said, "the reason you couldn't find an undo spell is because there isn't just one spell that will undo any other spell. All spells have to be unraveled individually, usually by creating some kind of opposite of the original spell. So if your shrinking spell used fire, you might use ice for an unshrinking spell. Maybe."

"That doesn't make sense." Brent waved his hands in the air to get Isabel's attention. "Some reactions are irreversible—everyone knows that. You can't unburn toast by putting it in the freezer."

"Excuse me, little boy, whoever you are." Marisol leaned forward so that Brent had to stare straight up to meet her eyes. "Are you a bruja? A witch?"

"No, because—"

"Are you an expert on magic?"

"Magic doesn't—"

"Then I don't care how many fourth-grade science textbooks you've read. Keep quiet and learn something."

"Be nice, Marisol," Isabel scolded. "Brent, magic operates by rules, just like everything. The rules just happen to be different from the rules of the physical world. Scientists study the physical world, but brujas study the magical world, and after years of spell casting, we've managed to figure out what a lot of those rules are. And we know what we're talking about."

Brent shrugged. Marisol poked him with a long red fingernail. "Ow, okay, I'm sorry."

"Anyway, Leo, one of the good things about being a beginner is that it's easy for your more experienced teachers to undo your spells, so you don't have to worry about creating opposite unraveling spells for every little mistake you make. I'll show you. Do you have a piece of ribbon? Or a string would work," Isabel said.

Leo looked around her room. She probably had something that Isabel could use, somewhere. Maybe left at the bottom of her sock drawer or buried in the wooden chest of dress-up clothes and board games at the foot of her bed.

"Here." Marisol held out her hand, which had just been empty. It now contained a piece of silky red ribbon about as long as Brent was tall.

"Thanks." Isabel took the ribbon and tied it quickly into a long line of knots, one on top of the other. She handed the knotted ribbon to Leo. "Now tell us what happened, and don't leave anything out. It's part of the spell."

Leo told them. She did her best to focus and concentrate so that her story became threads of magic twisting into the knotted ribbon.

". . . and so I took him home and put him in the dollhouse and fed him a quesadilla, and I need to get him back soon before the police catch us!"

"And before my mom tears the town down looking for me," Brent added. Marisol hushed him with a one-fingered tap on his head.

"Thank you, Leo." Isabel took the knotted ribbon back and raised her eyebrows. "You have been practicing, haven't you? I can feel it in your magic. Okay, scoot back, everyone. Give him some room." Marisol and Leo moved to the very edges of the bed, leaving tiny Brent alone in the empty space of the center. Isabel held out her hand to Marisol, who took it with a slight eye roll. Then Isabel closed her eyes, and the knots in her palm melted away, leaving a straight length of red ribbon.

"There you go, Leo." Isabel opened her eyes with a smile. "Now let's get your friend back to—" She stopped, her mouth hanging open.

"It didn't work," said Brent in his same squeaky voice, in his same shrunken body. "Why didn't it work?"

"I . . . um . . ." Isabel fiddled with the ribbon, as if checking to make sure no knots were hiding in it. Leo couldn't remember if she'd ever seen her older sister look so confused.

"Did you screw it up?" Marisol asked. "He should at least have turned a weird color or something if you screwed it up. Why didn't anything happen?"

"I . . . don't know," Isabel admitted.

Leo had been in near-panic mode for such a long time, she was surprised that she even noticed her pounding heart or churning stomach or tightening throat anymore. But fear was hard to ignore, creeping through her and freezing her organs and brain. What if Brent was right after all? What if some reactions, some spells, couldn't be unraveled? Leo had been so relieved to turn everything over to Isabel, to let someone else fix things, it never occurred to her it might be unfixable.

Isabel, Marisol, and Leo stared at each other

in hopeless confusion, and might have gone on staring—except that right then the door creaked, and three pairs of eyes peeked around the open crack.

CHAPTER 25
SÉANCE

"Hey, it's a party," said Alma.

"Nobody invited us," said Belén.

"Meow," said Señor Gato, leaping straight back onto the bed and settling into Leo's lap. He made a point of ignoring Brent and licking his front paws, as if he had never been interested in pouncing on the small human in the first place.

"Close the door," Isabel told the twins. "We have a . . . situation."

"Hello." Belén approached the bed and held out one finger for Brent to shake. She turned to Leo. "Were you going to warn us about the danger of those cookies?"

"It wasn't the cookies." Leo dropped her head. "I was going to tell you about those—ask you, actually—but I got distracted. . . ." She leaned down to pull the Ziploc full of gingersnaps out from under her bed. "Are these safe to eat? They didn't shrink Brent—they just made him love everyone."

"Those are the love bites?" Isabel asked. "As long as you set the recipe to work on a specific person, anyone else who eats the results won't have side effects." Isabel's shaky voice grew stronger as she returned to her role as know-it-all. "And personally, I need all the sugar I can get." She grabbed a cookie from the bag and took a bite, chewing slowly and closing her eyes. "The undoing spell didn't work," she explained to Alma and Belén. "I don't know why. I'm afraid we're going to have to get Mamá involved, so you two might want to stay away. Keep out of trouble."

"That's all right." Alma shrugged. "We knew Leo was cooking up a love spell, so we're already conspirators. Plus we might be able to help." She and Belén edged their way onto the crowded bed, tucking their legs under them to fit. "Remember, we can go over Mamá's head."

"Do you think you can ask?" Isabel's voice squeaked and her eyes pleaded. "Is Abuela nearby? I'd like to talk to her."

"She's usually hanging around somewhere," Belén said. "But I haven't seen her in the house today."

"Can you call her?"

"We'll try to get a summoning going. Let's see, we'll need a candle—" Marisol held one out, a short white tea light in a tin holder. "And matches?" Instead, Marisol produced the purple lighter. "Thanks. Brent, do you mind moving out of the middle of the circle? That's sort of where the ghost is supposed to sit."

Brent's wide-eyed confusion matched Leo's feelings perfectly. He scrambled over the comforter to hide behind Leo, who lifted him into her hand to hide her surprise. She didn't know Alma and Belén could summon ghosts the way people did in scary movies that Leo wasn't supposed to watch. Although she liked the idea of getting advice from her abuela, Leo couldn't help but shiver at the idea of a séance. She looked down at Brent. "Do you want me to put you back in the dollhouse?"

"There's . . . there's no such thing as ghosts . . . ," Brent said, but he didn't sound entirely sure of himself.

While Alma and Belén set the candle in the middle of the bed and whispered to each other, Leo deposited Brent onto the third floor of the dollhouse, half wishing that she could hide with him and half excited to see the twins' special power up close.

Alma adjusted the candle the tiniest bit to the right when Leo returned to her spot on the bed. Belén scoffed, moved the candle barely to the left, and lit it. Leo's lights went out, which by now she expected. Alma and Belén, sitting across from each other at the head and foot of the bed, reached to hold hands over the flame. Their shifting made the small candle wobble, and Leo hoped that she wasn't about to set her bedroom on fire. Just in case, she planned her route to grab Brent and Señor Gato and get out of the room.

"Leonora Elena, what are you dreaming? Aren't you going to say hello?"

Leo jumped. Sitting—no, actually, *standing* in the center of the bed, her body from the waist down disappearing through the mattress, was Abuela. Small and wrinkled and hunched, she wore a purple dress and white sweater with a thin gold-chain necklace, like she was dressed up for church. Her white hair was pulled back in a bun, and she would have looked as sweet as cotton candy if it weren't for her eyes, which had the force of black holes and were currently turned disapprovingly at Leo.

"Sorry, Abuela!" Leo squeaked. "Hello. It's good to see you." And it was. Leo had been small when Abuela died, but seeing her now felt familiar and happy, not like a scary movie at all. It was like when Leo's grandma Logroño called to video chat from Florida. Even though they were separated, Leo always felt glad to hear that her grandma loved her, and to get to say that she loved her back. Plus her laugh sounded just like Daddy's when Leo told jokes.

Alma and Belén had dropped hands. Belén's eyes shone white like marbles.

"Well, you've all grown so much." Abuela's eyes turned softer as she looked around the circle, and Leo felt herself relax. "I peek in, of course, but you're always changing so fast. Oh, well, you didn't call me here to hear about your growth spurts, I guess. What's going on, hijas?"

It wasn't until that last word that Leo recognized the strangest part about talking to her dead abuela in her bedroom. Leo could understand her!

"Abuela!" Leo said before her sisters could answer Abuela's question. "You don't speak English."

Abuela gave Leo a stern look. "Leonora Elena, that was rude. I have had time to learn many things since you last saw me."

"Sorry." Leo hung her head.

"Poor Leo," Marisol snickered. "She never learned to deal with you, Abuela. Leo, here's a tip. If she tries to give you a lecture, just cover your ears and stick out your tongue. That always worked for me."

Abuela's laugh was loud, and it moved like an earthquake through her whole body. The sound tickled the back of Leo's brain like the first notes of a familiar song. "You were a little terror then, and I bet you're no better now, Marisol, mi sinvergüenza. Don't listen to her, Leonora."

"Abuela!" Alma bounced a little on the bed like she had transformed into the excitable seven-year-old she had been when Abuela was alive. "Don't you want to see what Leo did?" She pointed straight at the dollhouse.

Leo cringed.

Without ever moving through space, Abuela suddenly stood right in front of the dollhouse and peered straight in through the third-floor windows. Leo heard a strangled squeak, and felt sorry for Brent, who just a few minutes ago hadn't believed in ghosts.

"And who exactly are you?" Abuela put her hands on her hips. Leo guessed that she was probably giving Brent a very powerful glare.

"I . . . um . . . um, I'm Brent."

"Hmph." Abuela leaned even closer to the dollhouse. Then she turned and looked straight at Leo. "Well, Leonora, this doesn't look good at all."

CHAPTER 26
ABUELA

Leo tried to give her abuela the short version of how Brent had been turned into doll-sized Brent. She wanted to pass quickly over her many mistakes, and she also rushed for the sake of the twins, who were beginning to look noticeably strained from maintaining the séance. Alma's bouncing had gotten worse, a constant jiggling and fidgeting that made the candle flame wave dangerously, and Belén's face was shiny with sweat, the skin around her white eyes turned dark like she hadn't slept in weeks. Leo didn't know exactly how long they could keep Abuela here and visible, but it seemed to be wearing them out. No wonder they didn't do this for all the customers at the Día de los Muertos festival—passing voice messages was probably enough work.

"I thought it would be a pretty simple fix." Isabel took over the story with just a hint of pout in her voice after Leo recounted her failure, "but the unraveling spell didn't work at all. And I'm not sure what else to do, since . . . well, Mamá hasn't exactly taught me individual spell reversal yet."

Marisol snorted, and Isabel shot her her meanest look, transforming into a stretched-out version of Abuela.

"Mamá *told you*," Marisol said with a satisfied smile, "that you didn't need any more encouragement to try complicated spells you weren't ready for."

"Settle, girls," Abuela chided when Isabel opened her mouth to respond to Marisol. "Leonora, let me ask you something. Do you know why fifteen-year-olds have to be initiated into the family magic before they begin training in spell craft?"

Leo shrugged and inspected her comforter. "Alma and Belén aren't fifteen yet."

"By a few months, you're right, but they had your mother's permission and guidance, and they went through the initiation ceremony, as each girl must do before she can start practicing magic."

Leo shrugged again.

"Many people in this world have magic," Abuela said. "But they can use it in a hundred different ways. Some people become curanderas, using their magic to heal the sick. Some become alchemists or wizards and pull on the threads of the universe. Some people carry a more subtle magic, and never know what force leads them to dance a beautiful ballet or design dazzling skyscrapers. Your father's family has its share of latent magic, and he carries plenty of his own, though he doesn't know anything about it. It likes to hide, your father's magic."

Leo looked at her sisters. Except for Belén, who still stared straight ahead, they all looked surprised too, so it would seem Leo wasn't the only one who knew nothing about Daddy's magic.

"Many people know how to use brujería to connect their magic to the world using candles and herbs and faith and tradition. But what our family did— what your five-times-great-grandmother did—was find a way to understand her own magic, to make it grow, and to share it with her daughters. It made her stronger, and it makes each of you stronger too."

"How?" Leo asked. "How did she do that?"

"She became una bruja cocinera." Abuela winked

at her. "And she used her magic to unite her family."

"A kitchen witch," Isabel whispered.

"And for generations our family has passed down our witchcraft," Abuela continued, "each mother initiating her daughters into the family magic at fifteen. Though of course you broke tradition from the beginning, Leonora Elena—a fifth daughter."

Leo opened her mouth to ask Abuela more about her birth, and about her birth-order magic, but Abuela shook her head and waggled a finger at Leo's face.

"The initiation ceremony is very important for a new bruja. During this ceremony, the initiate's magic joins with the family magic, the magic of her sisters, her ancestors, and her descendants." Abuela paused until Leo lifted her guilty eyes out of her lap and met her grandmother's gaze. "The ceremony allows for other members of the family to combine their magic with the new bruja's magic, to work joint spells, lend strength, and even undo a spell cast by another family member. Before this joining, the new bruja's magic is more distinctly her own, and she alone can use or unravel it."

"You mean we can't help her. Leo has to undo the spell herself." Isabel covered her mouth with her hand.

Abuela nodded. Leo's heart pounded. Isabel and Marisol stared. Alma and Belén fidgeted.

From the dollhouse, a high-pitched groan broke the silence.

"I'm doomed," Brent moaned.

CHAPTER 27
THE PLAN

Leo put a hand out to settle Alma, whose fidgeting had turned into an almost-constant shaking. It was easier for Leo to worry about her sister than it was to face the pit of anxiety that had spread in her stomach. *She alone* . . . Leo working alone had started this whole mess, and now she had to work alone to fix it.

The worst part was, Leo had wanted this. She'd wanted to be the center of attention, wanted her sisters to stop pushing her aside and talking over her head. She'd wanted to use magic to make herself special and important.

No wonder all her spells had gone so dramatically wrong.

"Are you all right?" Leo asked Belén, whose skin was clammy when Leo patted her arm. "Should I get you some water?" Belén shook her head but didn't speak.

"Girls." Abuela held out a hand, and Leo hesitated before reaching to take it. The ghost flesh was as solid as it looked, though it felt light and disconnected, as if Leo held a disembodied hand. "I should leave before your sisters drain themselves. But I so enjoy seeing you all. Leonora Elena, if you want my advice, talk to your mother. She can help. And good luck. You can do this. Don't listen to that old dirty cat."

Señor Gato, who had been slinking toward the dollhouse with his rear in the air, turned around and meowed sweetly.

Abuela kissed each girl on the cheek and patted Alma and Belén on the head. "Que bueno trabajo, hijas. Gracias. God bless!" And she was gone. The candle flame sputtered and died, and Leo blinked in the light of her ceiling lamp.

"Girls?" Mamá's voice called from the living room. "Where is everyone? There are still dirty dishes in the sink."

Leo froze. In spite of Abuela's advice, Leo still couldn't imagine anything worse than the anger and disappointment Mamá would have for Leo if she found out about all of this.

"You're not planning to tell her, are you?" Marisol whispered.

Leo shook her head, her eyes glued to the tea candle that was little more than a puddle in its tin casing by now. Mamá would smell the candle smoke, or the magic, and she would storm in here and figure everything out, and then she would never teach Leo to do magic, and Leo would never work in the bakery. She would have to get a job doing the most boring thing in the world, like taxes, or writing the labels for soup cans.

Leo didn't want to write the labels for soup cans for the rest of her life!

"Right." Marisol stood up. "I wouldn't have been any help with the magic stuff, but I can keep Mamá and Daddy busy while you work on it. Good luck, cucaracha. There's the old hamster cage in my room if you need somewhere to keep your little friend." She slipped out of the room before Brent could get out more than an outraged yelp.

Leo heard Mamá, her footsteps clicking up the hall, stop to ask Marisol what was going on. "Isabel is a horrible brat and I hate her!" Marisol screamed in response. "And I don't know why I even bother staying in this house when everyone would be happier if I just left! Maybe I'll drop out of school and run away to New York and make a living as a street magician!"

Mamá followed Marisol's stomping back down the hall, away from Leo's room. The soft tones of Mamá trying to calm Marisol and the sharp tones of Marisol refusing to be calmed continued, promising to keep attention away from Leo's room. If she hadn't known that it would ruin the act, Leo would have run down the hall to give Marisol a giant hug.

Belén tried to stand, and swayed a little with one hand propping her against the bed. Alma, who was still twitchy but more stable, offered her twin an arm. "We're going to go grab some ice cream," she said, smiling while chewing on her lip. "And maybe more quesadillas. Or a cookie. Lots of cookies could be good. Do we have any more lemon bars?" Belén perked up at the mention of food, so Alma towed her twin toward the door. "I'm sorry we're not being more help, but . . ."

"You're worn out." Isabel shook her head. "You already helped so much. And you heard Abuela, anyway. Leo's on her own."

"Yeah . . ." Alma reached up to flatten her already-flat pink bangs. "Leo, you've already done more complicated spells than Belén and I have. Don't worry. We know you can do it." Her fidgeting didn't make her look entirely trustworthy, but Leo was glad for the kind words anyway.

"Okay, little Leo," Isabel said once the room emptied out. "Here we are again."

Leo remembered sitting in the bakery office, looking up at Isabel and hearing for the first time about magic and sweetness and brujas. The beautiful blizzard spell Isabel had shared. Leo wondered if Isabel regretted ever telling her anything at all.

Even though everything had gotten so messy, Leo didn't regret learning about magic. She only regretted not learning more, and now, hopefully, she would fix that. Leo took one deep breath and held it until her stomach stopped churning.

"So I need to make an unraveling spell. And I have to do it on my own. But I don't know how."

"I can help you with that. Mamá won't let me practice them yet, but I did my own research on the theory of how it's done."

Leo smiled. At least one sister understood Leo's sneaky magic learning.

Isabel read over the honey-jar recipe with Leo, explaining how each ingredient needed to be replaced with its magical opposite in order to make a working undo spell. It was a tricky task.

"You had the right instincts with your first love potion, taking out the target so the spell would work more generally. But you also saw how a change like that could have unintended consequences."

Leo nodded, and gulped. There were so many different ingredients in the honey jar. If each one had a possibility of failing as badly as Leo's other experiments, maybe this reversal spell wasn't such a good idea.

Brent had the same fear. "I don't understand why you can't just tell Leo which ingredients to use for the . . . process," he gulped, apparently not quite willing to use the word "spell." "Leo could still be the one to actually put it together, but why does she have to make up the whole thing?"

"I just told you. Unraveling spells are finicky. The spell that shrank you was Leo's—her mind, her magic, her mistakes. No reversal spell I invented, or even one Mamá or Abuela invented, would work perfectly."

But what was the opposite of honey? Or a

spiderweb? Leo felt like her brain was being overkneaded until it was tough and flat and pummeled. "How can I pick? Everything could be wrong."

"It's not about being right or wrong." Isabel's voice remained patient, even though her fingers kept tugging nervously at her ponytail. "It's about making sense to you and your spell."

If Leo hadn't been so grateful for her sister's help, she might have been terribly annoyed.

Leo decided on molasses to be the base ingredient for her opposite spell. Molasses was sweet and thick and would create a jar with a consistency like the original spell, but it was dark instead of light and man-made instead of natural, and it reminded Leo of winter instead of spring. Instead of a spiderweb, the spell would use a cut piece of the silk Leo had accidentally stolen from the cabinet—material made from insects, thin and shiny like a spiderweb, but coming from a protective cocoon instead of a misleading trap of a web. In place of candy hearts, Leo chose chocolate coins, because of their association with luck—Leo felt like this spell needed all the luck it could get. Finally, she decided to use leaves from the giant oak tree in their yard to replace the lilac bonsai leaves.

She wrote it down on a sheet of notebook paper.

LEO'S ANTI-SHRINKING JAR SPELL
TO GROW A BOY NORMAL SIZED

INGREDIENTS

1 glass jar
1 faucet of running water (for purification)
molasses, enough to fill the jar
silk cloth
lucky chocolate coins
leaves from a giant oak tree

Isabel helped Leo sneak into the kitchen and gather her ingredients. Instead of using a candle, Leo washed the jar in the bathroom sink to get rid of the leftover honey and also to purify with water instead of fire. She blew into the jar, laid down the silk, poured the molasses, and dropped in the chocolate. She thought about freedom, about breaking down the old spell, about protecting Brent from all the out-of-control magic he'd had thrown at him.

After consulting with Isabel, Leo also added a crumbled-up piece of a leftover Love Bite gingersnap, and a scrap of paper that Brent hesitantly wrote his name on with the smallest pencil Leo could find. This, Leo hoped, would erase the effects of the first love potion, if any were still lingering.

There were only two steps left to the spell, both of which required leaving Leo's room. But a bad feeling made her pause. She was missing something, she felt sure. Something was wrong.

"You're nervous. It makes sense. But we don't have much time, Leo, so get out there."

The sun had fully set, and the moon peeked through the window behind the dollhouse. Marisol had resorted to muffled sobbing in the living room, and both Mamá and Daddy were focused on her supposed crisis, which Alma and Belén kept popping into Leo's room to report on. Brent had fallen into a restless nap on the doll bed, and Señor Gato had given up trying to pounce on the visitor and resorted to hiding under the bed, watching the dollhouse, and meowing. The molasses jar sat on the floor in front of Leo's bed. Things were not quite normal, but Leo couldn't identify anything that should be making her feel so strongly that she was forgetting something.

She only remembered when she turned her wandering gaze to her bookshelves.

"Can you wait here, please?" she asked Isabel. "And watch everything? I just need five minutes. Also, can I borrow your cell phone?"

Leo felt like an escaped prisoner as she crept

across the hall to Isabel and Marisol's room, where the cell phone was plugged in and placed neatly on the edge of Isabel's carefully ordered desk. Leo woke it up, dialed the number ripped out of her notebook, listened as it rang.

Caroline answered her phone with a cautious "Um, hello?"

"It's me," Leo said. "I'm calling from Isabel's phone."

"Leo!" Caroline's voice morphed from soft to piercing. "What is going on? You hung up without telling me anything."

"I'm sorry." Tears rose in the back of Leo's eyes. "I'm really sorry. I—"

"You know," Caroline said, cutting Leo off, "you complain about your family not trusting you, about keeping secrets and lying. But from what I can tell, you're the biggest liar of all!"

Leo's heart sank. "I . . . I know. You're right, Caroline, but . . . Isabel's helping me now. I asked her to help."

"Good," Caroline snapped. "I told you to." Her breath huffed and crackled through the phone. "Did . . . did she find a solution?"

"We found something I can try," Leo said, but her heart sank just thinking about the plan. "I don't know if it will work, though. And I've messed everything up so badly so far, and . . ."

Leo was afraid. She was afraid that she would never find a way to fix Brent. She was afraid of getting arrested and of Mamá being angry with her and of her sisters growing up and learning magic without her. She was afraid that, even if her unraveling spell worked perfectly, it was too late. She was afraid Caroline wouldn't want to be her friend anymore, no matter what happened.

"Hey." Caroline's voice came out softer after a long pause. "Leo, it's okay. I'm sure you can figure it out."

Leo shook her head, even though her friend couldn't see her. How could Caroline have any faith left in Leo after how horribly everything had gone?

"I shouldn't have called you a liar. And I know you can do this. Do you know why? Because you"— Caroline interrupted herself with a laugh—"you are the most talented witch I know."

Leo sniffed. "Because I'm the only witch you know, right?"

Caroline laughed some more. Leo decided that her friend had cracked under the pressure of the past few days.

"I'm sorry," Leo said again. "I'm sorry for pulling

you and Brent into this."

Caroline sighed. "I'm sorry for wanting to get pulled in. But you know what's better than an apology? A solution."

"Okay." Leo took a shaky breath. "I'm going to go try the spell now. Wish me luck."

"Good luck, Leo," Caroline said. "I really do believe in you."

Leo hung up the phone, feeling better in spite of the tears in her eyes. The bad feeling of forgetting something had disappeared, and Leo remembered that Caroline had been a part of the original spell. Even if she couldn't be here helping with this opposite spell, at least she knew about it, and was wishing Leo luck. That had to count for something.

Leo replaced Isabel's phone and scurried down the hall toward the front door to get the final ingredient.

CHAPTER 28
UNRAVELING

When Leo snuck out the front door, Marisol's tirade showed no sign of ending. Leo made it outside and left the door ajar while she tiptoed across the dark lawn, moisture from the ground seeping into her socks.

The tree in the middle of the yard spread tall and wide, with a trunk as big as a refrigerator and branches that shaded most of the house. If there was ever an opposite of a bonsai tree, this towering oak was it. The leaves weren't changing colors yet (it usually took until almost Christmas for that), but Leo found a fallen leaf without too much trouble.

She carried it inside, back to her room, where Isabel chatted with Brent, asking what his favorite classes were (science and English) and what he planned to do for Thanksgiving (visit his dad and stepfamily in Dallas).

"There you are." Isabel smiled at Leo, and her voice held the same pleasant tone she had used to talk to Brent, but from the way she pressed her lips together and tugged at the hem of her blouse, Leo knew her sister was nervous. "Did you get what you needed? Are you ready?"

"I got it." Leo thought of the phone call with Caroline more than the leaf she clutched to her chest. "Let's go."

She dropped the oak leaf into the jar. Isabel plucked Brent out of the dollhouse and carried him to the bed.

"Have either of you ever had to swim in something sticky?" Brent eyed the jar with a frown. Leo and Isabel shook their heads. "Well, it's not fun. It feels horrible in your clothes." He had changed back into his pajamas, still damp, and he shivered a little in his bare feet.

"The sooner you're big, the sooner you can get home to your mom," Isabel reminded him.

He nodded. "This had better work."

Amen, Leo thought, scrunching her eyes to send her prayer up faster. She tried to concentrate, to pour a little more magic into the molasses jar, to make it work. Everything counted on her doing this spell just right, and she was terrified.

But then she remembered that Caroline believed in her, that Alma and Abuela believed in her, that Isabel and Marisol and Belén believed in her or they wouldn't have been helping her out all night. And she managed a tiny smile, and a nod, and Brent let go of her finger and cannonballed straight into the molasses mixture.

After two full seconds, Leo reached in and fished Brent out by the back of his T-shirt, set him on the washcloth that Isabel had laid out, and licked the molasses off the tips of her fingers. Brent swiped the dark syrup out of his closed eyes and away from his lips. Isabel sat like a statue, not even breathing.

Leo gulped. "Why didn't it—"

With a noise like a firecracker, tiny Brent exploded up and out. The jar, which had been sitting just a few inches from him, rocketed away so hard it cracked against the wall, splitting into two pieces that dripped gooey molasses onto Leo's pillow. But the mess didn't bother Leo, because sitting in the middle of her bed, still covered with molasses and sputtering as he adjusted to the explosion, was Brent. Normal-sized Brent in normal-sized Spider-Man pajamas, wiping a normal-sized bucketful of molasses out of his hair.

"That"—he blinked at Leo through molasses-sticky eyelashes—"was highly unscientific." A giant grin spread across his face as he stretched his arms above his head and took stock of his back-to-normal body. "I guess you really are a witch."

"Actually," said a voice from behind Leo, "she's a bruja."

Mamá stood in the doorway, her face slowly shifting from worry to anger. Behind her, Daddy's face was stuck in total shock. Marisol hung back, giving a helpless shrug. Leo gulped.

"And this little bruja," Mamá continued, "has a lot of explaining to do."

CHAPTER 29
BRUJA

The next hour felt like eating a slice of cake on a too-full stomach. Watching Brent smile into the phone, calling Caroline to share the good news, seeing Mrs. Bayman run from her car to hug her son without even noticing the leftover streaks of molasses rubbing off onto her clothes—the triumph of the moment was rich on Leo's tongue. But behind her, Mamá fumed like a stomachache.

They didn't make any particular plan. Brent told his mom that he had snuck out and spent the day in the park, and that he had walked to Leo's house because it was closer than home. Leo could see a hundred holes in that story—starting with the question of why Brent would sneak out in his pajamas with no shoes—but luckily Mrs. Bayman was too relieved and happy and angry to ask any more questions. Mamá didn't talk much, but she did offer hot chocolate and gingersnaps to the Baymans. Brent, for maybe the first time ever, declined the cookies.

Once Brent and his mom disappeared down the dark street, the house was too quiet. Leo shifted from one foot to the other, waiting for someone to say something. Instead, Daddy and Mamá moved slowly toward the kitchen, and Leo and her sisters trailed anxiously after them, settling into seats around the table without a word.

Usually, Mamá's anger came out through her mouth. When she got annoyed or disappointed, she might click her tongue, sigh, lecture, or just say Leo's name in that defeated tone of voice that all moms seemed to practice. When she really lost her temper, like when Marisol snuck out of the house after being grounded, Mamá could yell louder and faster than anyone, never seeming to stop for breath. But now, when Leo had broken a hundred rules, had sneaked and lied and stolen and almost gotten herself arrested, Mamá was silent. Leo's stomach twisted in knots.

"Leo." Daddy sat at the head of the table, glancing every few seconds toward Mamá. "Did you steal ingredients from the bakery?"

"Yes." Leo's voice came out as a whisper.

"Did you steal ingredients to practice magic spells that you shouldn't know anything about?"

"Yes."

Around the kitchen table, Isabel picked away invisible bits of imperfection from her cuticles, and Marisol used her thumbnail to press crescent-moon-shaped scratches into the wooden tabletop. Alma and Belén, still exhausted from summoning Abuela, sipped mugs of hot chocolate and twitched their eyebrows at each other wearily. But no one's silence was louder or more unsettling than Mamá's.

"And then you cast a spell—a spell you knew nothing about, a spell you knew you shouldn't be messing with—on that boy from your class?" Daddy sighed. "I'm just trying to understand . . . why, Leo?"

"I was—" Leo started.

"It was my fault," Isabel interrupted. "I was the one who told her about magic. I showed her spells."

"We encouraged her," Alma added. "We knew she was making cookies for Brent and we asked her to report back to us. We basically told her to do it." Belén nodded, and added, "We would have told her anyway if Isabel hadn't. It's not fair that everyone else knew and she didn't."

"I didn't stop her when I knew she was experimenting," Marisol fessed up. "I told her to cut it out, but I didn't do anything. It's kind of an unfair rule, making everyone wait until they're fifteen. We should get rid of that. Leo would make a better magic student than me, anyway—"

Mamá stood up, her chair scraping against the linoleum floor, silencing the flood of defense. "Enough," she said. "Leo, go get everything you stole. Bring it out to the car. You need to return the ingredients to the bakery, and we need to have a talk." Marisol and Isabel started to stand up too, but Mamá stopped them with a look. "Alone."

They drove in Mamá's minivan down the mostly empty streets of Rose Hill. Leo sat in the front seat with her backpack on her lap, packed full of the spell ingredients and the recipe book. The car stayed quiet, and the quiet was suffocating. Car rides with Daddy might include long stretches of silence, but Mamá usually chatted away. When Leo peeked sideways, her mother's face was smooth and flat, and Leo couldn't tell what thoughts hid behind it.

But she could guess. *Irresponsible,* Mamá was probably thinking. *Reckless and sneaky and disrespectful.* Leo shrank into her seat.

A million years later, they pulled up to the bakery. Leo climbed out of the car, backpack over her shoulders, and followed Mamá through the back door and into the bakery kitchen.

Everything was dark and cold and quiet. Mamá flipped the office light and nodded for Leo to sit in Daddy's chair. Leo squinted at the clock on the wall (she'd never mastered reading the nondigital kind) and worked out that it was already 10:25, way past the time Mamá went to bed, since she would have to be back here at 4:30 in the morning to open the shop. The realization that her mischief would keep Mamá from sleep was the very last bit of guilt Leo could handle. Tears prickled the back of her throat and started to leak into her eyes. She sniffed.

"What's wrong?" Mamá sat in her own chair across from Leo. "'Jita? What's the matter?"

"It's late," Leo whispered, since it would come out like sobs if she used her voice. Her chin wobbled and her nose scrunched and her eyes filled slowly with water, but she refused to cry.

"Leo," Mamá said.

Leo looked up and felt one uncooperative drop

spill over the edge of her eyelash.

"Sweetie, what were you thinking?"

At first Leo thought this was the beginning of Mamá's lecture, but after another long silence, she realized that she really wanted an answer.

"I was trying to fix things." Leo brushed away the tear, even though she was sure Mamá had already seen it. She wanted to explain herself without tears. "I was trying to fix the shrinking that happened because I was trying to fix the love spell that happened because I was trying to fix things for Caroline." Mamá looked confused, but she didn't ask for more explanation, and Leo was tired of telling the story over and over anyway. "I found out that we have magic, and what's the point of having magic if you can't use it to fix things?"

Mamá didn't give an answer. "Do you have everything you stole?" She pointed to Leo's backpack under the chair. "Take it all out, please."

"I didn't steal it all on purpose. I was just trying to get the spiderwebs, but it all came off the shelf together." Leo pulled out the strange items and spread them across the floor.

"There it is." Mamá reached for the object wrapped in dark silk. Leo had cut a corner off the silk, but the bundle remained intact. "This is important, 'jita.

You shouldn't have taken it. You shouldn't take anything without permission, especially magic things."

"I know." Leo sighed. "I'm sorry."

"I hope you are, because we're not going to keep any more secrets from each other, either of us. Agreed?"

Leo blinked. It almost sounded like Mamá felt bad too. "Agreed," she said.

Mamá nodded and started unwinding the silk. "I'm upset that you didn't come to me, Leo, when you first had questions about magic. I'm upset that you relied on stolen books and guesses even when the first spell went wrong. And I'm so sad that when you got into real trouble, you tried to hide it from me."

Leo sank into the cushion of Daddy's chair, tapping her fingers and trying not to cry more. She had known all along that she was being bad and sneaky, but she kept doing it anyway, which was the worst kind of bad and sneaky.

"But mostly I'm upset because I know where you learned to be so secretive. I'm sorry for keeping things from you." Mamá pulled away the last layer of silk and exposed a small chunk of chalky white rock, about the size of a jagged marshmallow. "Now hold out your hand. I want to test something."

Leo held out her hand automatically, stunned by Mamá's apology. Without ever touching the rock herself, Mamá lifted the silk and tilted it into Leo's palm. The overhead lights flicked off, their glow replaced by a bright white glow coming out of Leo's hand. The rock hummed, shooting out light in flickering bursts.

"What is it?"

"That crystal belonged to your great-great-grandmother. It measures the strength of a person's magic. And that light means you have a lot more magic than most fifteen-year-olds when they begin their training."

Leo fought the urge to move the stone so she could itch her palm. "Why?"

"Well"—Mamá shook her head slowly—"I don't really know, 'jita. It might be because of all the illicit practicing you've been up to. It might be because you're mature for your age, or because your Mamá is such a powerful and talented bruja that she rubbed off on you." Mamá winked. "Or it might be because, ever since you were born, you've always been determined to keep up with your sisters, no matter what."

Leo smiled at the light in her palm. Its glow reminded her of a candle, flickering slightly and giving off wisps of the cinnamon magic smell. "So if I have all this magic, what do I do with it? What . . ." She thought about Isabel's and Marisol's argument, about Abuela's advice. "What does it mean to be a witch?"

"A bruja," Mamá corrected. "A witch can be anyone. A bruja is us. And what does it mean to be a bruja?" Mamá smiled. "That's like asking what it means to be a Texan, or a girl, or curly haired. It doesn't mean anything by itself. It's part of you. Then you decide what it means."

Leo nodded, even though she didn't quite understand. "So what do I do now?"

"You have to be trained. As soon as possible. I'll start scheduling you for shifts here at the bakery like your sisters, so you can have lessons. That includes lessons on how to run the cash register, help with inventory, boring stuff like that, as well as the spells, okay? If you're here, you have to carry your weight."

Leo nodded, but something deep in her stomach flickered in time with the glowing crystal. Something felt not right about this. Too easy.

"That's it?" she demanded.

"What's it?"

"I get to take magic lessons and I'm not in any trouble at all?"

Mamá hesitated. "I'm not happy about what you did, Leo, and I really wish you had trusted me enough to talk to me. But . . . well, I understand, sort of. You're growing up, figuring things out. When I was your age—"

"Mamá! I am not a little kid," Leo groaned. "If Marisol or Isabel stole things from the bakery, you would yell at them, or ground them." Leo dropped the crystal into its silk wrapping and blinked as the office light came back on.

"Do you want me to ground you?" Mamá asked with something that looked suspiciously like a smile hidden behind one hand.

"Yes," Leo snapped. "I *shrank* Brent Bayman!"

"Okay, okay." Mamá held up her hands in surrender. "For how long?"

Leo thought about it. "How long would you ground Marisol if she did something like this?"

"Hmm . . . probably a week. Do you want to be grounded for a week?"

"One week? Alma and Belén were grounded for one week just for skipping school one day with no magic."

"Two weeks?"

Leo paused. Two weeks was a long time to go without visiting Caroline's house or watching TV.

"Two weeks is fine, I guess."

"All right, Leonora Elena Logroño. You are hereby grounded for two weeks for sneaking and borrowing and spell casting all without permission. I'm very disappointed in you."

Leo frowned at Mamá. "You don't sound very disappointed."

"I am. I really am. I'm just distracted by how proud I am that you cast a full reversal spell all by yourself."

Leo beamed. "Mamá, you're supposed to be mad about that."

"Oh, I'm furious. And if you ever try to keep such a big secret again, you'll be sorry. I'll give you dinner that makes all your hair fall out the day before class pictures." Leo laughed, and Mamá touched her cheek. "I'm serious, 'jita—now that you know about magic, you're not safe from any pranks. You've opened the door for some very creative parenting."

Leo chuckled, and it felt good to let her stomach unwind itself with a loud belly laugh. No more disasters, no more secrets. "Mamá?"

"Mm-hm?"

"How soon can I start learning new spells?"

"You'll have to be patient, because we need to

initiate you. I'll have to ask Paloma to wash the robes. . . ."

"Mamá?"

"Yes, Leo?"

"I love you."

"I love you, too, amorcita." Mamá stood up, checked the clock, and yawned. "Now help me put away these stolen goods, and let's see if we can get home before midnight."

CHAPTER 30
BRUJA COCINERA

It wasn't Friday, but since Thanksgiving break started on Wednesday, the snack club had planned for their meeting to take place during this lunchtime. Leo passed around a plastic container of oatmeal-cranberry cookies that Isabel and Mamá had helped her make the night before. María Villarreal offered blob-shaped sugar cookies slathered with super-sweet pink frosting.

The entire sixth-grade class crowded around the table to taste the cookies, and plenty of seventh and eighth graders lingered nearby in case of leftovers. Mai, who turned out to be just the organizer the club needed, reminded Tricia and Emily Eccles that they were due to bring something delicious on the Friday after break. Leo looked around the cafeteria table, grinning hugely, amazed that the club had become a success so quickly. She caught Caroline's eye across the table and made a cross-eyed monster face. Caroline, who was busy stealing Brent's cookies whenever he turned his head, stuck out her bright-pink tongue and giggled.

Mamá only let Leo put a very tiny spell on the oatmeal cookies, a good-luck charm so simple that it hardly felt like real magic at all. But Leo grinned as she watched her friends and classmates eat, glad that the cookies carried a charm. She wanted everyone to have a happy, lucky holiday.

"Leo, your club cofounder is behaving very unprofessionally," Brent complained, reaching for another oatmeal cookie after Caroline passed his down to a waiting eighth grader. "Some of us aren't getting a chance to snack at this snack club."

"Oh, hush. She's going to give you all the leftovers at my house, anyway," Caroline said. "You're still coming over, Leo, right? My dad needs to ask you questions about the pumpkin pie we're supposed to bring to my grandma's."

"Yep!" Officially ungrounded now, Leo couldn't

wait to spend the crisp afternoon on Caroline's trampoline. "But I have to leave by five. I have . . . that thing at the bakery."

"What thing?" Brent asked.

"Oh, right." Caroline winked exaggeratedly. "The thing."

"What right? What thing?" Brent looked nervous. "Leo! It had better not be the kind of thing I think it is. I thought you weren't going to do that kind of thing anymore."

"Actually," Leo said with a smile, "today is my official initiation ceremony into the *family business*. After today, I'll really start learning the thing."

"You mean . . ." Brent's groan was muffled by a mouthful of cookie.

"That's right." Leo licked a dollop of pink frosting off her finger and smiled at the sweetness. "I'm just getting started."

"Cookie cutters!" Leo cried. "Mamá, where do we keep the cookie cutters?"

The Saturday morning sun peeked through the bakery windows, and Leo's time ticked away. Only one hour until the bakery opened.

"I'll get it, Leo." Isabel dug through one of the cabinets while balancing a tray of unbaked bolillos.

Marisol and Mamá worked in the front of the bakery, decorating the front windows with Christmas wreaths and colorful lanterns and paper stars. Tía Paloma and Isabel filled and emptied the big ovens in the back of the bakery. Alma and Belén quibbled over the perfect arrangement of goods in the display cases.

In her own corner of counter space, Leo separated a fistful of her dough and rolled it out flat on the floured surface. She liked the weight of the dough in her hands, and the smell of flour and ginger and molasses. Leo had developed a fondness for molasses.

The cookie cutter was solid and silvery and almost as big as Leo's hand, and she pressed it into the rolled dough and lined the shapes on her waiting tray until it was full—a dozen perfect puerquitos, ready for baking.

"How do they look?" Mamá peeked over the swinging blue doors to check on the back of the bakery.

"Perfect!" Leo hoped her answer was true. She still wondered if she had added just a little too much flour, or if she had grated the hard cone of piloncillo sugar fine enough. She checked her recipe for the thousandth time, squinting at the familiar cursive on the faded index card.

Mamá joined Leo at her workstation and kissed

the top of her head. "Good work. You're not sleepy, 'jita?"

Even though she had woken up at four, Leo didn't feel at all sleepy. Excitement buzzed through her. For the first time, Mamá's bakery staff schedule included Leo's name.

"She's doing a lot better than I did on my first day." Marisol leaned against the swinging doors and yawned. "Or on any day. In fact, since she's doing such a great job, I nominate Leo to take all my shifts from now on."

"Do you want me to pop those in the oven?" Isabel reached for Leo's tray.

"No, wait!" Leo spread her arms to protect her cookies. "I . . . um, I haven't finished the egg glaze. I'll do it."

"Mamá!" Alma called from the front of the bakery. "Tell Belén you can't mix chocolate croissants with regular ones in the display. Everyone will get confused."

"No, they won't, because the chocolate ones are covered in chocolate," Belén snapped.

Mamá hurried away to settle Alma and Belén, trailed by sleepy Marisol. Leo leaned over the tray and smelled the pigs. She kept her eyes shut and her head focused until the spicy scent tickled her nose.

Then she added the finishing touches, brushed beaten egg over the tops of the cookies, and slipped the tray into the oven before anyone could see.

"Have you finished memorizing the table of herbal ingredients?" Tía Paloma asked after Leo added her next two trays of puerquitos to the oven line. "I can give you a quick quiz."

"No boring stuff on her first day." Marisol appeared behind Leo and tweaked her carefully slicked-back ponytail. "Come on, Leo, I need help setting up the nativity."

Leo didn't think her magic lessons were boring, but she wanted to avoid a quiz. (Ginger and cinnamon both amplified magic, Leo remembered, but was it heather or lemon verbena that strengthened protection spells?) Tía Paloma shrugged and winked, and Leo let Marisol drag her to the front window, where she unpacked the nativity figures for eleven and a half minutes until the ding of a timer signaled that her tray was done.

"I'll get them!" Leo leaped to her feet and almost knocked the angel off the stable roof.

"Don't worry, 'jita. I've got it," Mamá called. "They smell wonderful." Leo dashed into the swinging doorway just in time to see Mamá set the tray on the counter and lean over it with a smile. "These look perfect, Leo, really. Oh, um, but these ones in the back, what do they have— *Oh*."

With several tiny pops, the six winged cookies shot off the tray and sailed over Mamá's head. Two invaded the front window, making Marisol yelp and shoo them away. Two knocked against Alma and Belén's display case, trying to reach the pan dulce inside. One settled happily on top of the miniature Christmas tree in the corner. And one, the cookie from the very back of the pan whose thin back leg had baked a crispier dark brown than the rest of its body, hovered around Leo's head, crumbs falling into her ponytail.

While Mamá chased the naughty cookies and Tía Paloma laughed, Leo held out her palm for the burned puerquito. "Hello, bonita," Leo whispered. "Welcome to the bakery."

The cookie spiraled into the air, raining happy cookie crumbles. Leo bounced with joy at the completed spell, the morning sun, her bustling family, and the sweetness that tied them all together.

Leo's Lucky Pigs didn't actually fly off the shelves, but they sold so quickly that Leo stayed busy, baking all day long.

LEONORA LOGROÑO'S
LUCKY RECIPE BOOK

**LOVE SUGAR
MAGIC**

LEO'S LUCKY PIGS

Makes 24–28 cookies. Be careful, because these little things fly.

INGREDIENTS

1¾ cups dark brown sugar, firmly packed

¾ cup water

1 cinnamon stick

½ pound unsalted butter cut into small pieces, plus a little extra for greasing the pan, then left at room temperature

2 tablespoons honey

4¼ cups all-purpose flour, plus a little extra for dusting

1 teaspoon baking powder

1 teaspoon baking soda

½ teaspoon salt

2 large eggs at room temperature, lightly beaten

1 large egg for the glaze, lightly beaten

powdered sugar for dusting

DIRECTIONS

In a medium-sized saucepan, combine the brown sugar, water, and cinnamon. Bring to a simmer over medium heat. Lower the heat and simmer until the brown sugar has dissolved and the liquid thickens to a light syrup. Turn off the heat and remove the cinnamon stick. Add the butter and honey and stir the mixture until they're melted.

In a large bowl, whisk together the flour, baking powder, baking soda, and salt. Create a well in the center of the dry ingredients and pour in the brown sugar mixture. Fold in with a spatula until well combined. Add two of the eggs and stir. The dough will be very sticky.

Place two long pieces of plastic wrap over the bowl so that it is completely covered. Carefully flip the bowl and let the dough fall into the plastic wrap. Scrape out any remaining dough. Wrap up the dough and refrigerate for at least two hours.

Preheat oven to 375 degrees F. Butter two cookie sheets. Sprinkle flour on work surface. Using a rolling pin, roll out the dough to about ¼ inch thick. Use a three-inch piggy cookie cutter and press it down on the dough to cut out the cookies. Gather the scraps and roll out again, then press out more cookies until all the dough is used.

Transfer cookies to the prepared cookie sheets and space them out. Gently brush the cookies with egg to glaze. Bake in batches for 7–9 minutes. Remove from oven and transfer to rack. Sift powdered sugar on top of the cooled cookies.

PAN DE MUERTO MENSAJERO

Makes two loaves. One bite will connect you with those who have passed on.

INGREDIENTS

FOR DOUGH

½ cup butter, plus a little extra for greasing the bowl

½ cup whole milk

½ cup water

5 cups flour, plus a little extra for dusting

2 packets of active dry yeast

1 teaspoon salt

1 tablespoon of whole anise seed

½ cup sugar

4 eggs

FOR TOPPING

½ cup sugar

¼ cup unsalted butter

2 tablespoons of grated orange zest

⅓ cup freshly squeezed orange juice

DIRECTIONS FOR DOUGH

In a saucepan over medium heat, place butter, milk, and water and heat until it's warm throughout (about 105 degrees F), but not boiling.

In a large mixing bowl, combine ½ cup flour, yeast, salt, anise seed, and sugar. Slowly beat the warm milk mixture into it until it is well incorporated. Add the eggs, one at a time, mixing throughout.

Slowly add in another 1 cup of the flour. Continue adding the additional remaining cups of flour slowly until the dough is soft but not sticky.

Put the dough onto a lightly floured board and knead for at least 10 minutes or until smooth and elastic. Form the dough into a large ball. Lightly grease a bowl with butter and put the dough inside it. Flip the dough around inside the bowl so that the grease coats it.

Cover the dough loosely with plastic or a cloth, and then let it sit and rise until it's doubled in size. It will take approximately 1 to 1½ hours.

After the dough has risen, punch it down, then shape it into two loaves, first pinching off four smaller pieces of the dough, two from each loaf; roll them out into cylinders. These are for your bones!

Lay your bones on top of the loaves in a crisscross,

one crisscross for each loaf. Set the loaves on an ungreased baking sheet and let them rise in a warm place until they double in size again. It will take another hour.

Preheat oven to 350 degrees F. Bake the bread for 40 minutes.

DIRECTIONS FOR TOPPING

In a saucepan over medium heat, combine ¼ cup sugar, butter, orange zest, and orange juice; bring just to a boil so the sugar is completely dissolved. Remove from heat. When loaves are baked, brush the glaze over them and sprinkle evenly with remaining half of sugar all over the top.

ABUELITA'S ALEGRÍAS (AMARANTH BARS)

Makes about two dozen. Gluten free, and guaranteed to get rid of unhappiness.
No oven.

INGREDIENTS

- ½ cup toasted peanuts
- ½ cup toasted pecans
- ½ cup raisins
- ½ cup toasted pumpkin seeds (optional)
- 8 ounces chopped-up piloncillo (panela)*
- ½ cup honey
- ½ teaspoon freshly squeezed lime or lemon juice
- 4 ounces puffed amaranth seeds

*piloncillo or panela is unrefined pure cane sugar

DIRECTIONS

Line a baking sheet with parchment paper. Mix together the peanuts, pecans, raisins, and pumpkin seeds. Spread the mixture onto the prepared baking sheet. Combine the piloncillo, honey, and lemon juice in a medium-sized pot over medium heat. Cook until the piloncillo has melted and the mixture has thickened, about 5 to 10 minutes. Stir a little to help the piloncillo melt. Turn off the heat and add the amaranth seeds. Stir the seeds quickly into the mixture, and be sure to mix well.

Pour this liquid onto the pan with the seeds and nuts. Wet your hands and press down on the mixture. Be careful not to burn your hands! Allow the sheet to cool completely for about 45 to 50 minutes. Transfer the mixture to a cutting board and cut it into bars or squares. If the mixture sticks to your knife, try dusting it with a little flour, or dipping it into hot water, drying it, and then continuing to cut.

Store the bars in a sealed container.

ACKNOWLEDGMENTS

This book would not exist without the love, sweat, and absolute magic of so many people.

Dhonielle Clayton and Sona Charaipotra at CAKE Literary, who trusted me with Leo before she was a person. Y'all have supported me through every step of this process and beyond, and I am so lucky to be part of the CAKE family. Can you believe the Logroños are here?

My agent, Victoria Marini: thank you so much for all the good advice, for great first-chapter saves, and for believing in me past this book.

My editor, Jordan Brown: thank you for loving what this was and shaping what it became.

Everyone who helped get Leo out of my head and into the real physical world, especially Debbie Kovacs and the team at Walden Pond Press: thank you for working so hard to make everything look like it's falling into place magically. I'm also grateful to Mirelle Ortega, who made the gorgeous cover and interior illustrations.

The YA lit community as a whole is so supportive and amazing, and I especially want to thank my New School professors Caron Levis, David Levithan, and Sarah Weeks, along with my Writing for Children cohort. Thanks also to Zoraida Córdova for being the cool older writer cousin I want to impress and emulate. I was extremely lucky to have Tehlor Kay Mejia, bruja extraordinaire and all around writing genius, as my sensitivity reader—thanks for all the work you do. And to all the 2017 debut authors and Electric Eighteens, thanks for the support, solidarity, and hysterical laughter.

I might never have met Dhonielle and Sona without the intervention of Kiki Chatzopoulou and Amanda Saulsberry. I never would have finished without their encouragement, or the help of my motivational-chart partner, Laura Silverman, and the world's fastest beta reader, Meghan Drummond. Y'all make me a better writer and person. Insert cheesy line from *Wicked* here.

My friends in Houston and New York, thank you for being so awesome whenever I needed to talk through drafting and editing. Claire, Devon, and Mary, I could never send an email or write a best-friend relationship without you. Andrea, thank you for answering a million middle-of-the-night Spanish questions. Ariel, thanking you for the translations, the research tours, the beta reads, and the pep talks still doesn't come close to covering it.

To my parents, Frank and Rita; my brothers, Michael and Gabriel; all the Meriano and Lynch aunts, uncles, and cousins, and Grandma and Grandpa, you all made it easy to write a family story. Everything I do is possible because of you. Love y'all.

And to my students and readers, thanks for listening. I really hope we're able to figure some stuff out together.